Simone Roncucci

Five Days With Me

Youcanprint *Self-Publishing*

Titolo | Five Days With Me

Autore | Simone Roncucci

ISBN | 978-88-93214-28-5

© Tutti I diritti riservati all'Autore

Nessuna parte di questo libro può

essere riprodotta senza il

Preventive assenso dell'Autore.

Youcanprint Self-Publishing

Via Roma, 73 – 73039 Tricase (LE) – Italy

www.youcanprint.it

info@youcanprint.it

Facebook: facebook.com/youcanprint.it

Twitter: twitter.com/youcanprintit

The water in the bottle first lulled slowly then faster. Sitting on a chair, Elizabeth rested her elbows on the kitchen table and her chin on her hands, looking spellbound at the water lulling itself, waiting until it finally settled.

Her mother cleared off the table. Elizabeth had eaten very little. The emptiness she felt in her "tight stomach" made her lose her appetite, but more than likely she had lost it for another reason: the breakup from her boyfriend.

On Valentine's Day, Anthony thought to give her a present. "Hi Elizabeth," he said on the phone, without having the courage to confront her directly," I'm sorry, but we can't see each other anymore, not now or forever. " As much as Elizabeth tried to explain what might have happened, her attempts were futile. So there Elizabeth found herself on lovers' day, staring at a water bottle from a dinner she had just barely touched.

"Come on, cheer up," her mother suddenly cried out, "When one door closes, another opens!" an expression typically said with the slight hope of lifting someone's spirit, but that usually went in one ear and out the other.

"Let's hope it hasn't become rusty" exclaimed Elizabeth with a weary voice, getting up from her chair, intent on giving her mother a hand in cleaning up the table. She seemed to see a frail spirit more than a person: she was tall, with long hair down to her shoulders or a little longer, thin enough to scare an anchovy, so much so that as she staggered to get up from her chair, she appeared to be a mere shadow of herself.

"Leave everything where it is. I'll do it. Just go and relax," said her mother to her daughter, who seemed very much in need of some relaxation.

Elizabeth walked uncertainly with her head lowered to her bedroom; she opened the door: a wardrobe and a bureau were there facing each other, and as old as they were, it seemed like they were telling each other the story of their lives. Awaiting Elizabeth in the middle of her bedroom was her bed, which she threw herself on without even pulling back the covers.

From her bedroom window, she could see the long branches of bare trees reach into the sky and a pair of turtle doves perched on a branch as if they were resting from a long trip.

She turned it on to see if there were any text messages for her, but the technological device stayed silent for about half an hour until a piercing, ringing sound notified her of an incoming text message.

Curious who it could be and what the sender wanted, she opened her mobile phone with one hand and pressed the button "read": it was Laura, one of her high school friends, who informed her that she was going to participate in a "five-day campaign", a sort of full immersion in the symbolic places of the area. Actually, five days spent outside, sleeping and eating in a camper in places near their city.

Elizabeth and her friends lived in Siena, a marvelous medieval city located in the heart of the Tuscany, geographically near the sea and the mountains, the countryside completely surrounded what had always been for Elizabeth her home, her life after having left Great Britain where she was born because of her parents' jobs.

It wasn't so much that she felt like going on that trip, but she thought that five days out with her friends wouldn't have hurt her emotional state, actually quite to the contrary.

She went over to her mother, who, in the meantime, had already finished cleaning up the kitchen and told her that she would be leaving in two days to embark on this new experience.

The following evening, Elizabeth packed her suitcase with everything she would need for the trip: two dresses, a hairdryer, some soap, a toothbrush, a pair of shoes, and some makeup in her beauty case, just in case. Usually, for many of us, once we have closed our suitcase, we expend quite a bit of energy to lock it up; even if we're only away from home for a few days. Even for Elizabeth, that's exactly how it went.

The following morning, hearing her alarm clock sound, Elizabeth woke up, all excited for the days to come spent with her friends: it was six in the morning: the sun had just timidly peaked over the horizon. An occasional turtle dove could be seen from her window and some gusts of wind swept away paper on the street. She had a hot shower and a light breakfast, and then after saying goodbye to her parents, she took her suitcase, opened the door, and went down the stairs.

Her pace was not yet very certain. She was still sleepy, but her desire to leave was so strong, that before she knew it, she found herself driving her car, going toward Laura's house.

While she was driving, Elizabeth's imagination took off, just as she had; a thousand thoughts ran through her head like out-of-control race cars on a race track.

Elizabeth really loved writing and she always had a notepad and some pens with her to keep her thoughts and memories alive.

That morning, her mind was focused on the cosmic universe: "What is it" she thought. "Which was born first? Light or sound? If it's true that everything began with the Big Bang, the enormous explosion would have come from the blaze, thus light and immediately after, the bang thus sound; but what exploded, the nothingness or perhaps a material point existed that, fifteen million years ago, exploded, causing a series of chain reactions which created the universe that is still expanding, but also cooling?"

As she drove to her friend Laura's house, she thought about the beginning of time. Laura had already got out to tidy up the camper.

"How's it going Ely" said Laura suddenly as soon as Elizabeth had come closer to her; "Well, how do you want things to go? As always, only strange thoughts are keeping me company," she answered. She took her suitcase and put it in the camper, then she parked her car in Laura's garage, and together they waited for their friend, who arrived about ten minutes later.

"We can get on our way," Laura said, who got in the driver's seat, worrying if she had packed everything and locked the door to the house.

They got in the camper: a mobile home with three beds, a queen-size one and two twin ones, a table with four chairs, a narrow bathroom, a small, but spacious wardrobe and a kitchenette with its own gas tank.

They headed off to the sea.

To take full advantage of her camper, Laura came up with a five-day plan, which included spending one day at the sea, one in the mountain, one in the countryside, one in the abbey and the last one in town.

In essence, a quick visit of the most meaningful places in the surrounding area.

The road to the sea, which took about an hour from town, was full of curves and tight spots, but she and her friends didn't care one bit as they were used to taking it.

Sitting at the table, Elizabeth had already pulled out her pen and notepad: its pages were full of thoughts and aphorisms.

The first one she read she had found on a piece of paper hanging up on a wall at work. Struck by its beauty, she had recopied in her notebook,: "There are moments in life when you miss someone so much that you just want to pick them from your dreams and hug them for real." These words made Elizabeth think about Anthony and a big teardrop slid down her face.

"No, stop it," she thought to herself. "I left to distract myself, so no more strange thoughts."

She then read another quote she had written and that seemed more appropriate. When you were born, you were crying and everyone around you was smiling at you. Live your life so that when you die, you will be the only one smiling and everyone around you will be crying."

Now that was better.

After many curves and words exchanged with her friends, they arrived at the sea: never-ending beaches and pine woods lined a calm and relaxing sea.

They settled at a camping site. Once the camper was set up, they decided to throw themselves on the beach like children on their first day at the beach.

Sandy but happy, they headed off on a long walk, barefoot, even if the weather wasn't all that suited for it, but they thought, as anyone should, you only live once so let's live it up.

They reached the end of the pier, turned around, and walked back to the beach, leaving room for the boats to dock.

They sat down to admire the panorama: the seagulls were flying high behind the fishing boats, the wind blew as soon as the water, breaking on the rocks. It brought them the kind of soothing relaxation they had long since forgotten.

They went on the rocks and sat again to admire the sea.

From afar, they could see islands on the horizon, the sea sang with its waves.

Elizabeth, enthralled by nature's beauty, lied down as comfortably as possible and fell asleep within a couple of minutes, while her friends talked about this and that.

When they woke up, they decided together to go back to the camper because it was already lunchtime.

They bought some pasta and meat at a small, but well-stocked store on the campgrounds. They went back to the camper, and while one cooked, the others set the table.

Spaghetti with garlic, oil, and chili pepper, small steaks, salad, fruit, and coffee was what they had for lunch.

And naturally, after that, they took a break to let their food digest; each one of them lying in their own beds. They fell asleep, sleeping for almost two hours.

Once they woke up and cleared the table, they went back out for a walk, and on the rocks, they lit a cigarette, talking and telling stories and some fun-spirited jokes to make each other laugh.

Once they were back on the beach, they began playing with a dog whose owner was letting him run on the water's edge. It was so nice, like the rest of the day: so carefree.

Later that evening, they went to have an ice cream in town, and after, they came back to the campgrounds to make dinner and get ready for the next morning.

After dinner, in the faint light of the camper, they began to argue over a game of checkers, going on and ending that tiring day in any case; they made their beds and lied down on them, sleeping like logs until the next morning.

Since they had already paid for their camping place, they got up around six a.m., and after refreshing themselves, they headed off in the direction of the mountain.

Naturally not before having breakfast.

Laura at in the driver's seat of the camper while her other friends sat down to eat at the table.

Elizabeth, who was struck by the events of the day before, felt inspired to write about it. Being an avid writer, she took her notepad, her pen, and began to scribble down some notes on a blank sheet of paper.

The road was still long, about a little over two hours, and she took advantage of it by writing down a story to kill more time: she took a soda from the fridge and let her imagination run wild.

She wanted to write a story about the sea, love, and wanted her imagination to take flight. She thought up the title "High-flying Love" which seemed right and began to daydream.

Time passed, the kilometers passed by slow but decidedly, without resting as there was no need. The camper was filled with everything.

And Elizabeth wrote.

She didn't even realize they'd stopped to change drivers with another one of the friends, as she was caught up in her own world, and Laura certainly would never have dared to divert her attention from her creative hobby.

After driving a couple of kilometers more, Elizabeth closed her notepad, put her pen back in her bag, and went to stand in front of her friends.

"Finally," they said "Are you with us?"

"Excuse me, but when I get inspired, I have to write otherwise, forget about it," answered Elizabeth, satisfied with her barely-finished work.

"Here we are, everyone here is the mountain," said the driver, turning around.

Lush, green pastures, and fresh, sweet-smelling forests opened before their eyes.

Another one of nature's spectacles and….another campground.

They went in, proceeded to turn in their documents and be assigned their camping spot.

They took the cable car up the 2.000-meter mountain, bringing a picnic table and a few things with them.

Their trip in the cable car was slow, but steady; the landscape opened up in front of them from an impressively high altitude, as Laura kept herself busy for the entire ride, and she grasped the cable car rail, as if it would save her if something were to happen.

All of a sudden, down came a goat. How majestic it was. It seemed as if it appeared to greet them from the primordial rocks.

Wonderful.

They arrived, landing with a jerk at 2,000 meters above ground. The first thing to greet them was a frigid gust of wind and a snowy panorama. Thank goodness they brought their wind jackets.

They sat down on a clearing covered with trees from where you could see the town below and the mountain tops all around them. What superb air.

They set up the table, took out the chairs from inside it, and sat down to admire the panorama.

They were so enraptured by the view that none of them said a word. The only noise they heard came from a squirrel that ran away quickly into the forest.

After a little bit, they packed up the table and went for a walk among the green trees, paying attention where they placed their feet, seeing once again that very squirrel that had run away into the forest and farther away in the distance, a rock goat was jumping around, full of joy.

The fragrance of nature: unforgettable.

They headed out on a path that led them to a waterfall of pure, fresh spring water: they took small sips of it since it was freezing cold, and while they continued admiring the landscape, they noticed the water flowing quickly down the mountain.

Elizabeth silently admired all of it.

They returned to the footpath, took the cable car, returned to the valley and then went to the campground.

They heated up the camper, had lunch, took their usual walks in the park, and at dinnertime, they set the table as usual, and after, they all went to bed.

The morning after, early in the morning, they left the campground and said goodbye to the mountains.

Along the road, there were pastures: cows with cowbells and baaing sheep saying goodbye to Elizabeth and her friends.

And Elizabeth wanted to write again what she was feeling inside: The mountain had captivated her so much so that it felt as if her mind and her body had been carried away by a faraway wind to places never seen before.

So then she decided to entitle her new story "Alien Hurricane" as a new feeling began pervading her.

And then, as usual, she let her imagination run wild as they had a long trip ahead of them.

How wonderful, how fun, how important friendship is. Without them, she would have surely spent those days locked up in her house, feeling sorry for herself, and instead, they gave her a renewed passion and *joie de vivre*.

They slowly made their way back to their town, but they had not yet finished.

They had to go to the countryside.

And they arrived in the countryside, hearing a rooster crowing, and a bell ringing from a bell tower in a faraway town.

That day, they stopped at a small farm where a friend of Laura's lived. They would have to do without the camper.

After ringing the bell with a long chain, the doored opened, and out walked Mario, a dear friend of Laura's, a seventy-something-year-old man, dressed in velvet pants, a flannel shirt, and a straw hat.

"Come on in, make yourself at home," said Mario to his new guests.

They went up the stairs to go outside to a place that brought them to an arched terrace; they went inside and found themselves in a room: a big and spacious kitchen that was all the rage during the peasant period, with a huge table and two benches on either side.

Besides the kitchen, which had a fireplace where you could go and sit down next to, there was a long corridor with a bathroom on the right and some rooms on the left.

"Today y'all are my guests, but, everyone get to work," exclaimed Mario, smiling.

They began eating breakfast: pasta with tomato sauce from the night before heated up on the stovetop, two nice pieces of country bread with salami, cheese, and two big slices of onions, a glass of wine, and with a toothpick in the mouths, off they went to work on the land!

"Y'all have come now at a time when there's little work, but there's always ploughing to be done," said Mario smiling, who went to get the mules, and once he attached the plough using the "yoke", they began going up and down the field, plowing the terrain.

They spent the greater part of the morning ploughing the terrain: then came lunchtime (in dialect "*la desina*") and after having taken off boots shows and washing themselves with water heated in a pot over the fireplace, and a piece of yellow soap, they went in the house, where Mario's wife had already prepared a soup with vegetables from their garden, chicken with potatoes and "*nostrale*" salad and ham from the farmhouse cellar.

"Y'all had better eat everything, peasant life is hard, and if you don't eat, the land won't do the work for you," Mario often said, "I ground the ham and salami myself from the pigs you saw before while we were working with the mules. This year, the good Lord has given us plenty of wine and potatoes and the oil comes from those olive trees there. Try finding these things in town!"

And he was right.

They had never eaten such exquisite food at home: Life was completely different before: better and healthier.

There was no doubt about it.

When they heard the coffee pot on the kitchen stove whistle, they knew the coffee was ready.

Everything was so good. How was it possible?

The coffee, the water, the food, even the salad seemed to taste different. And maybe it did.

They drank coffee and smoked cigarettes together next to the lit fireplace (hearth), the wood burning continuously, served as a backdrop to the stories Mario told about life many years ago.

Later they all went together to feed the pigs, cows, hens, rabbits. It seemed like the best job in the world.

"Why don't I give you the food for the animals, just our leftovers," Mario went on saying. "That's why this is better. I don't put trash (junk food, conservatives, et cetera) in the food mix at all!"

Simply being with Mario was a hoot, like going fifty years back in time.

Feelings like none other.

"And I tied the wine with rope and put it in the well, that way it stays fresh" he went on saying.

The sun set behind hay bales in the countryside: the golden rays of the sun and its soft pink light lit up the house and their camper.

Elizabeth and her friends looked at each other, even their faces had been lit up by the golden, pink rays of the sun.

The world seemed to be burning like fire in a fireplace.

Yet another dinner with the usual of foods grown on the land, cooked as long as needed on the stovetop.

"Now let's get to bed, tomorrow y'all will leave, but I'll stay here because the land doesn't do the work all by itself." In the meantime, Mario went to the bathroom to wash up and he put on his pyjamas, hand sewn by his wife, multicolored and full of patches. Everyone headed for their bedrooms: big rooms with twin beds made with handwoven sheets made from cotton, hemp canvas, still made "in that very field" surrounding the house.

They were a bit rough, but they went right to sleep, since peasant life was so tiring.

And the next morning, the rooster acted as their alarm clock.

They got up and went to their own bathrooms; as they passed by the kitchen, they saw breakfast ready on the table (pasta and ham again) with a bottle of wine waiting for a "customer".

Mario had made breakfast for them and had gone out in the field to work; before going out with the mules. He had cut the grass and given hay to the animals.

They had breakfast, gave a hand to Mario's wife in cleaning up and went down the stairs.

From afar, a man with mules waved to them.

"See you soon," Elizabeth and her friends yelled, tears welling in their eyes.

They were about to get in the camper when they saw three small wicker baskets with chicken eggs and a notecard which said: "Thank you for your visit. It's nice to see people interested in the countryside. These eggs are a gift and a goodbye from not only us but also the animals. Hope to see you soon.

All three of them moved to tears, they left that world they knew as the countryside.

There's no use telling the thoughts that flooded Elizabeth's mind.

In fact, she started writing right away, she already had a new title for her new story; Rodothàr, an imaginative name she had had in mind for quite some time; she wanted to write a love story, a trip across the countryside, so she already had some ideas.

Now their new destination was a place of worship.

They decided to go to an abbey nearby, the magnificent Mount Oliveto Maggiore Abbey.

The abbey, located in a town near Siena (Closings n.d.r.), is the motherhouse of the Benedictine Congregation of Saint Mary of Mount Oliveto, founded by a sienese man, Beato Bernardo Tolomei (1272-1348).

The abbey, located in the center of the *crete senesi*, Sienese clay formations, in a place between the solitary and the wild, is a wonderful example of artistic and spiritual beauty.

They went in the abbey, having previously left the camper in the car park, and after going up the hill to the place of worship by foot, they crossed a drawbridge and went inside.

After going down the hill half a kilometer, they arrived in front of the magnificent Abbey, with its tower and a shop with monk-made products next to it.

They went in the church and listened to the Gregorian hymns that the monks began singing at certain times of the day.

It felt like they were in heaven: frescoes on the walls, silence and spirituality all around them and the Gregorian backdrop created a magic atmosphere.

Even if our friends here weren't all that religious, they loved to take a peak in these mystic places every once in a while.

It calmed and restored their souls.

And that's exactly what being in the church did for them this time.

They spent the rest of the day in silence and prayer, pausing a moment to understand themselves better: past, present, future.

That evening, Elizabeth had a sandwich for dinner while she was writing. This time, words, poems, and sentences came into her head more than titles.

She spent the entire evening writing, because, if she hadn't written then, she would have lost her creative inspiration.

The morning of their fifth day, she woke up the other two and they went on their way to their last destination: the city of Siena.

They arrived there early, seeing as it only took a few kilometers to get from the Abbey to the city.

They went to Laura's house, left the camper there, and got in Elizabeth's car. It would be easier to find a parking spot in the city.

They arrived in Siena, wandered around the city, explored its museums, and went to the Duomo, Siena's cathedral, Santa Maria della Scala, the old hospital the Baptistery, San Domenico church, and finally to Piazza del Campo, the main square.

They were very familiar with these places, having been to them many times in their lives.

After a visit to the town hall, they ended their trip with the fascinating view of the city from the Mangia tower, overlooking the shell-shaped square below and on the horizon…

On the horizon, mountains could be seen from afar, and even farther away,

Five unforgettable days spent with her friends.

The magic of friendship.

After a few days, the doorbell rang at both Elizabeth's friends' houses. It was the postman delivering a package.

They were the very stories written by Elizabeth, who thanked them for their sincere friendship with this kind gesture.

1. High-Flying Love

Leaving is a little bit like dying: an expression which doesn't always mirror the truth. It depends from case to case.

Cafal, a very normal, unpretentious person, had a similar case of leaving.

For her entire life she had been a blue collar worker with a big, loving and altruistic heart.

Her glowing eyes mirrored her noble soul within.

Cafal worked hard, at work as much as at home, the normal life, (but not too much) of a woman.

There was only one thing missing in Cafal's life: love!

Various bad experiences had led her to lead the life of a single girl. Much to her dismay, she had got used to it but had put up with it for too long.

Even if the days passed rather quickly, her heart and mind were already focused on her upcoming vacation where she would spend twenty days on a beautiful Greek island: Ettocs!

And finally vacation time came.

An airplace ticket, two suitcases packed full of clothes, and a great desire to relax saw off Cafal at the airport.

Cafal's small city, located in an unknown area in central Italy, had a small airport, but fortunately, it had a direct flight available to the place she was heading to.

Check-in time and after, finally, the speakers made a crackling sound, announcing that the plane was beginning to board for the island of Ettocs!

Cafal stood up, took her suitcases, and made her way to the boarding gate.

The airplane, a four-wheeled engine from the Alidan airline company, sporting an unknown color but very elegant, had all the necessary comforts: comfortable and roomy seats that looked like armchairs, reclining ones fitted in a rare, pastel blue fabric; nice, efficient hostesses; plasma televisions with surround sound!

A piano bar with live music was also available upon request: a keyboard which simulated a piano, a voice, and so forth…

Ettocs, here we come!

The airplane awaited the green light from the command tower to signal takeoff: it positioned itself in the middle of the track, and after being given the go ahead, it began to taxi, its engine roaring loudly.

Cafal looked out the airplane window at what now seemed to be a plastic version of her city!

The airplane flying at full power would reach its necessary height, and once it reached cruising speed, it would take Cafal's heart and soul to that island she so yearned to go to.

"I'm your commander Danval," said a voice suddenly. "Welcome aboard. We would like to inform you passengers that we are flying 5000 feet above ground at 300 km / h. The ground temperature is thirty degrees while the temperature outside the aircraft is ten degrees celcius. We are flying over the western coast of Italy, with the Pugliese coast on your right and the Adriatic, the coast of ex-Yugoslavia, on your left. The weather is nice. There is excellent visibility and no wind.

"This is your commander wishing everyone a pleasant flight!"

"Now, I feel like I'm on vacation!" exclaimed Cafal, reclining her seat back and stretching out her legs a bit.

"Would you like some coffee?" said a hostess with a cart full of steamy hot delicacies,

"Yes, thank you," answered Cafal, reaching out her hand to take a decorated porcelain coffee cup filled with steaming, premium black coffee.

They spent the last two hours of the flight watching a film: *Gone with the Wind*!

"Ladies and gentlemen please fasten your seatbelts," said the commander over the loudspeakers.

Quickly and decidedly, the hostesses helped the passengers get ready to land.

The island made itself out to be a piece of heaven on Earth: a long asphalt strip made it seem like it was the landing strip…the airplane, in fact, veering widely and moving it's flaps, got into position to land.

The sound of airplane parts coming from under their feet gave them the idea that the undercarriage was going down.

As they got ever closer, the landing strip began to take form.

Here it was…closer and closer, lower and lower…the engine's power had decreased considerably…three…two…one…Earth!

The aircraft still moved in such a way that it seemed like they were in a bus, and then, once it was still, the commander said: "Ladies and gentlemen, here we are on the island of Ettocs. As you can see, the weather is great and the temperature is thirty-two degrees: We at Alidan hope that we have provided you with the most comfortable flight possible and thank you for choosing to fly with us!"

A loud applause broke out in response to not only the announcement, but also to the smooth landing, free of turbulence. Perfect!

The door opened.

Cafal stood up, took her suitcases, and got off the plane.

Ettocs! How wonderful: a small green island, with crystalline seas, and mountain chains so high they could practically touch the sky.

There were polite inhabitants with multi-colored souvenir stands, full of island objects.

A taxi was already there waiting to take her to the hotel.

She got in, and off she went.

The hotel resembled Greek civilization: it was a huge building, the main entrance adorned with columns, marble, and granite.

She walked into an elegant reception with statues facing the main entrance, which brought ancient greeks to mind.

How wonderful the famous Greek myths were!

Once she left the documents at the reception, Cafal took the key from his bedroom: room number 3…"a perfect number," she thought.

She went up the stairs.

The bedroom door, a color between walnut and chestnut, opened with the first turn of the key.

A Grecian-styled bedroom: pink marble floors, a four-poster bed with an embroidered lace blanket, television, fridge, and a huge bathroom with a hydromassage bathtub so relaxing it would allow her mind to drift away, then another terrace faced the crystalline sea with white beaches and green trees framed what would be a sunny, once-in-a-lifetime vacation.

Excited to see the panorama around her, Cafal put her clothes up in the wardrobe, freshened up, and then off she went, to explore that enchanted place.

"Ah, finally!" sighed Cafal, breathing air different than the one she was used to, uncontaminated, dust and pollution free, and instead only breezes that carried scents of local flowers and sea salt to reinvigorate her mind and body.

She took a walk around the street markets, a memory to take back with her to Italy; she had a coffee in a bar and walked into shop after shop, where abundance reigned supreme.

For quite some time, Cafal wandered Ettocs' narrow streets; before she knew it, the time had already come for her to go back to the hotel.

From afar, she could see the columns of the renovated grandiose palace, the hotel where Cafal was staying.

Here I am, she thought when she arrived there. .

After a quick relaxing bath in the hotel bathroom, she got changed to go down to dinner.

"Goodness gracious, look at all this food!" Cafal thought to herself: the tables were nicely set, and in the center of the room, there was an enormous table with raw and cooked vegetables, an endless array of starters, first courses, second courses, and both surf and turf!

"Make some space, my dear tummy…but not too much; it's fine to indulge in a guilty pleasure, but it's not worth it to overdo it," thought Cafal, who had a big appetite in any case! She indulged herself in some coffee and dessert to end that unmemorable meal.

A far cry from the diets Cafal was used to doing!

After dinner, they were free to take a walk or wander in the hall to listen to relaxing live music.

Cafal chose to take a reinvigorating walk on the beach, not so much to admire the language as to digest the hearty dinner she'd just had.

But….what a beach it was!

The sound of waves beating against the rocks…the moonlight reflecting off the white sand, stars dotting the endless night sky!

How wonderful it all was!

Cafal walked up and down the beach a bunch of times, but no matter how many kilometers she walked, she still didn't feel anything in her legs since she was so enthralled by the beautiful natural landscape surrounding her.

The time came for her to go back to the hotel.

Her legs felt a bit tired since her daily routine had not accustomed her to taking long walks.

Thank God her hotel room was on the first floor!

She opened the door to her hotel room, walked in, and threw herself on the bed, where she went out like a light and where she woke up early the next morning.

"I fell asleep dressed, without even changing my clothes. I was wiped out" sighed Cafal while she went to the bathroom to do her daily washing up.

She went downstairs for her usual breakfast: coffee, milk, tea, and juices along with pastries and cookies with a variety of jams, everything already prepared "homemade" by the personnel.

Oh how fun!

An excursion to the top of the island with a small aircraft called a Cessna had been planned that morning.

After thanking the minibus driver who had given the visitors a ride up the local airport's small airway track, Cafal headed off on the small minibus and surprise!

The aircraft pilot who had taken Cafal to Ettocs was the very pilot of the Cessna who would take her up above the island: the commander Danval!

Cafal stood with her mouth wide open.

She hadn't seen the commander before, only his voice she had heard, but now he was there, right in front of her. A ray of sunlight struck her, her heart was beating fast. "Oh, but he's wonderful," she exclaimed, with a tone of voice higher-pitched than one she would have wanted to use.

Danval heard what she said, and he too found the sight of Cafal to be bright and one-of-a-kind.

They boarded the rolling aircraft and ready, set, go: take off!

The island seen from above was breathtaking: smooth white sand coasts reflecting in the sunlight that sunny day, green forest and clear seas, reflecting from far below the aircraft's shadow.

Now all of that became the second order of business!

The first one now was Danval!

Taller than she, he was a fine-looking man with a gaze that made her dreamy.

What a man Danval was!

They talked about this and that, the island, life, ancient Greek civilization, until a "loose" ticket made its way from Cafal's hand to Danval's.

The flight lasted about half an hour.

Danval took a ticket out of his pocket while Cafal was already getting on the minibus to take her back to the hotel: "Hotel Zeus room number 3 name Cafal," which was written on a small piece of paper with nice, rounded handwriting.

Excited, Danval decided to pass by the hotel that same evening to take Cafal out to dinner.

And he did exactly that.

He asked the hotel receptionist to call for Cafal in room number 3 to let her know that he had arrived.

Not even ten minutes later, a beautiful vision appeared!

It was Cafal, elegantly dressed, with eyes brighter than the earrings she was wearing. She went down the stairs to the hall where Danval, his mouth wide open, was waiting.

Seeing such a beauty walk down the stairs made it seem as he were seeing a movie star.

He couldn't believe how beautiful she was!

Cafal approached him; excited, Danval took her hand, and kissed her saying: "You're as luminous as the moon. I can't believe my eyes!"

Moved by his words, Cafal thanked him.

They left the hotel and headed toward Danval's car.

They went to dinner.

What a place, a restaurant overlooking the sea, as if it were something from a dream, those stars and those white beaches were reflected in the moonlight.

The candles burning on the table lit up their eyes, their hearts beat hard during that wonderful, moonlit evening.

They had dinner and then took a walk on the beach.

First, he touched her delicately on the shoulder and then on the hand, then:

Lightning struck!

Perhaps the magic atmosphere around them had been an accomplice in making that evening so romantic, or perhaps it had been two lovers meeting or perhaps both. Danval hugged Cafal tightly, and kissed her, making Cafal his, as he himself already felt she was.

It really was love!

The rest of the vacation went by, as if something out of a dream: light and carefree.

Now Cafal was happy.

As the days came to end, so did their vacation!

Now what would happen?

Danval said that he would follow Cafal and that soon they would get married!

That Alidan-airlines four-engined airplane took Cafal and Daval back home. (Instead of piloting the airplane, Danval who said goodbye to the island he had flown over year after year but now had come the time to say goodbye to it for good.) "So long, Ettocs, thank you for everything. Thank you for introducing me to Cafal. You will stay in my heart forever," he said with teary eyes.

They flew back quickly to that small city in central Italy. It took wide turns to get itself into position to make a perfect landing as it had always done.

"Here is your commander speaking. Thank you for flying with us and hope you have had a pleasant flight. Alidan airlines hopes you'll be flying with us soon!"

Danval left together with the passengers, took Cafal by the hand, and together they headed off toward what would become their house, leaving that much-loved airport behind them!

Cafal and Danval's house was their love nest. The night before, hand in hand, eye in eye, they had their first candlelit dinner together, and after, Cafal played a piece on the piano.

And like all love stories:

Cafal and Danval lived happily ever after!

2. ALIEN HURRICANE

Hamilton: Bermuda's capital.

A wonderful place with about 74.800 inhabitants immersed in the green earthy islands.

Frank Isolarb and Rita Minzon, researchers at the local Institute of Genetics: sinister building located in a place hidden by vegetation.

Frank and Rita, friends for quite some time now, had worked together at the institute for about four years.

Their friendship blossomed way back in 2002 when they began to meet each other to do various researches and genetic manipulations for their final thesis as genetic research students at the University of Cambridge.

Two entirely opposite personalities: one a nice, gentle technology lover and the other a strong, determined art lover.

However, at work, both of them were hard-headed and armed with a patience not typical of most people.

He was going through a rather strange period in his life, having left his entrepreneurial girlfriend in the hospitality sector and thrown himself wholeheartedly into his work; Rita, on the other hand, had grown accustomed to not worrying all that much about the company surrounding her, always concentrated on phials and freezing embryos.

And in a fairytale place: Bermuda.

In the capital, life went on as usual: the tourist destination attracted visitors all year round,   since the dry hot weather allowed winters to reach twenty-one degrees and summers twenty-nine degrees; all sorts of thriving recreational activities on the white beaches; sporting events such as sailing and surfing on the heavenly island waters.

Frank and Rita were assigned to go there for work. Italy, their native country, did not offer many career opportunities, and as it often happened, they found themselves having to choose between career and family.

Together they decided to pursue career opportunities, promising themselves that they would go back to Italy as soon as they had made a name for themselves in the genetics field, their work, their passion.

The genetics center in which Frank and Rita worked was located in an area hidden by greenery in the island back country: a circular building, built at the beginning of the 1950's, with a long tree-lined street as the only passageway.

The inhabitants of the area, the majority of them black or mixed-race, with few groups of whites, couldn't easily see the city center: the going of strange sealed vans going to and from the city center itself; access forbidden by all unauthorized persons, an area completely surrounded by walls and alarm systems; decontamination of vehicles heading into the facility.

There are also those who had sworn they'd noticed strange lights, somewhere between a light and a deep blue, radiating from within the center.

The researchers knew of these people, and they didn't make a big deal about it because they knew what type of work they were doing: why the decontaminations, alarm systems, and sealed vans were used.

And the lights were simple ultraviolet lamps used to disinfect the sterile places during the night.

For this very reason, the inhabitants of the surrounding areas couldn't know about these things.

"Rita, the wind has been blowing faster and faster for fifteen minutes now. Let's put those test tubes away and get out of here," exclaimed Frank suddenly.

He had already taken off his sterile lab coat and was waiting for Rita, who, in the meantime, was finishing putting embryos in the test tubes to then be put in the nitrogen container.

"I'm coming, I've almost finished. Wait for me in the office," she answered.

Frank sat in the director's armchair and waited.

He could sit in the director's armchair because Professor Snowin, the research center director, was in Italy for a convention, and Frank was enthusiastic about it, since he could use the office whenever he wanted to!

Frank sat comfortably in the armchair, watching Rita on the monitor as she closed the nitrogen containers: "She is so beautiful," he thought.

There had always been a certain attraction between the two of them, that out-of-body experience, but that had never blossomed into an actual relationship: there had never been any rhyme nor reason for their love to bloom.

It hadn't turned into anything yet.

Or maybe destiny had other plans for them.

Rita left the cleanroom and headed for the changing room for a refreshing shower.

After a few minutes, she appeared, before Frank's very eyes, all dressed-up, in all her glory: well-dressed and well-groomed, having paid attention to even the smallest of details.

Rita was a wonderful girl: not very tall, a little over four feet nine inches, weighing no more than 100 pounds, all of which made her look like a pretty little girl.

"Here I am. We can go to dinner!" Rita exclaimed as she took the keys to close and enter the center alarm.

Frank stood up and took his brand name jacket in one hand, an Italian brand that he loved very much and left the room with his colleague.

They closed the sealed center door and activated the alarm.

They left.

A half an hour later, they stopped at a quintessential restaurant of the island: a place with a sea view from a classic "pointed" roof.

They ordered dinner rich in fruits and vegetables, like that of good Bermudian cuisine. They chatted about life and this disgraceful world: societies full of hate, war, deforestation, abandoned animals, the crazy climate.

Not to mention the crazy climate.

The evening newscast was just announcing strong rainstorms on the horizon and a hurricane was taking shape on the hot waters of the Gulf.

Hurricanes aren't all that common in Bermuda, but they are highly likely to hit the island, given the short distance from the sea currents and places like the Bahamas, where the hurricanes would often hit with all their destructive force.

But there was nothing to worry about.

Their dinner passed by as they talked about such issues as these, Rita's face still in front of his, her face slightly lit by the feeble candlelight flickering on the table.

Wonderful.

Once they had finished dinner, they paid the bill and they head out for a walk around close by, just to get a taste of that piece of heaven that nature offered in all its magnificence.

"Look, clouds on the horizon. I don't like this one bit!" said Frank. "That wind especially, coming from that direction, doesn't look good," as the sky above them thundered louder.

"We'd better go home. I don't want to get drenched tonight!" said Rita, who looked for her car keys in her purse in the meantime.

They got in the car and once she had taken Frank back home, they said goodbye to each other as they made plans for the next day; working at the same place, they took turns using the car: first Rita, and then Frank

Frank went inside his house and turned on the t.v.

He wanted to have more news of this natural disaster, being the technology lover he was, as he was really interested in tracking systems.

In his house, he had installed one of those wind speed detectors, complete with a moisture meter and other technological features; he began to look at the various facts that were being collected on his computer, and he studied the cloud formation using the satellite images and checked wind pressure with the wind tracking sytem he had placed on the roof of his house.

Knowing the facts of the situation didn't calm him down one bit: on the gulf a thick cloud had formed with winds blowing at 80/90 km/h, according to the Beaufort scale, it classified this phenomenon as a Beaufort 10 thunderstorm, with very high long-crested waves, strings of seafoam came together to give the sea a whitish appearance. Low visibility in the sea.

"Let's hope all goes well," he said.

Fatigue and the late night hour had the upperhand; Frank headed towards his bed, where he fell into a deep, refreshing sleep.

The following morning, at 7 o'clock, Frank was awakened by his usual, annoying alarm.

Today, it was his turn to go pick up Rita at her house.

He took a refreshing shower, even though he didn't feel like it, and after breakfast, he went to Rita's house.

On time as always, Rita was ready and invited him in her house for a coffee.

Frank went up to Rita's apartment. Still half asleep, she poured Frank and herself a cup of steaming black coffee and they sipped it to allow themselves to wake up.

"Let's go, it's time to go," Rita announced.

They left the apartment, got in the car, and headed toward the research center.

On their way to work, Frank shared the facts regarding the cloud formation to Rita; "I've just realized it's raining!" said Rita with a smile: "Why would I have brought an umbrella?"

Their laughter enveloped the car cabin.

"We have to put the containers away in a safe place today, that way in case there is a problem, we'll feel more at ease," said Frank.

The weather got worse: gusts of wind and sinister-looking clouds covered Hamilton.

Once they got to the center of town, they deactivated the alarm and they went inside: they heard the wind beating hard against the windows.

They got changed and they decontaminated before going into the sterile room.

Rita began to put genes in the filials to then be put in nitrogen containers while Frank, worried, began to move things from the room to the ground floor to a specific basement. The other containers were ready to be sent away as soon as the anti-contamination lead van arrived.

There were about 20 containers, which were all heavy; Frank had to place them on a cart and put them one by one in the elevator to send them down to the safer underground floor.

After a couple of hours, he went back upstairs for a coffee and to see how Rita was coming along, and if she needed anything.

He turned on the computer and connected to his home network to check the weather conditions: he couldn't believe his eyes!

A level-three hurricane had already begun forming, but what was worse was that it was getting closer and closer to the Bermuda coast.

He turned on the center t.v. to find out more news: the great majority of the population was about to be evacuated.

"Rita, listen to this!" he said and plugged in the speakers to listen to the audio recording, there in that sterile environment where Rita had been working.

Blaring from the speakers, they heard, "Attention everyone living on the coasts, this is Noaa, American oceanographic agency speaking: Hurricane Rifran has now reached category five strength. The main damages caused by winds greater than 250 kilometers per hour have been overturned buildings and broken glass, exit ways blocked 3-5 hours before the strongest part of the hurricane hit, evacuate all residents; all residents must be evacuatd 8-16 kilometers along the coast because the waves have reached heights greater than 6 meters.

"I don't think we'll be able to get out of here and get to safety in time" said Rita.

"Close all open containers, and help me stow them away in a safe place!" said Frank, who, in the meantime, was running around looking for another cart to help Rita.

Rita closed the containers, and once she left the cleanroom, she began to help Frank with the cart and the remaining containers.

An hour after Frank had plugged the speakers in, it was announced that the hurricane had reached a low point and that it had slowed down its pace.

"We have a couple of hours before it hits here!" said Frank loudly: by then the sound of water and wind had become too loud for them, who ran around yelling to make themselves heard.

"Frank, all the containers don't fit in down there. We have to use the other basement room, but we have to get out of here!"

"Let's do it as fast as we can, it will be like hell here before we know it. Let's be quick!"

They loaded the containers on carts. Frank opened the door to go into the building next door where there was a second basement room.

"Rita, you can't see anything here outside, it's pitch black, the clouds and the rain have made everything dark; I'll try to make it out!" Frank yelled to Rita.

"Be careful, Frank, I'll prepare the other cart in the meantime!" she answered.

Frank went inside the building next door and placed the containers inside, left and struggled to return to the center: "We can't get out of here. You can't see anything. Let's take cover!"

"Let's go downstairs," he said suddenly to Rita. "We'll be safe until the storm passes!"

They closed the bolted door, unplugged the lamp to avoid short circuits, and using a flashlight to light their way, stowed them away in the basement, which was accessible through a security door where two stairways went down to a safer room.

 Hell didn't wait to make itself heard.

From where they were, Frank and Rita heard Rifran passing above: thunder that seemed like bombs, waterfalls rushing down, wind blowing…it was so windy: that hellish sound that destroys everything in its path: the voice of the devil!

The sound of broken glass, falling furniture, some leftover containers that were flung against the walls.

"Thank goodness the center is cone-shaped, the hurricane can wrap itself around it completely, but it can't damage it too much; the pointed roof can't be lifted!" said Frank, with a lump in his throat.

Frank and Rita looked around them: the dark room they were in enveloped them like a nest. The lit flashlights created a strangely warm and safe environment. They felt relieved, even though they were very afraid.

Thirty minutes, maybe more, went by, there in that room, time stood still.

At a certain point, they only heard silence, a strange and mysterious silence.

"We can go back upstairs, but we have to be careful; it isn't over yet!" said Frank.

They went upstairs, paying attention to where they stepped.

"Don't plug in the cord. It's not wise. Let's see what'll happen," exclaimed Frank, worried.

Luckily, there were only a couple of remaining containers, with glass and furnishings everywhere, the window coverings destroyed, the secured door had withstood the hurricane, but what would happen next?

"Why is it so hot in here?" said Rita while Frank ran to turn on the emergency light to use the computer.

"I don't have the slightest idea. Now let's see what the equipment says!"

"But weren't we not supposed to turn it on?" said Rita. "Yes," said Frank. "But I definitely have to check the nitrogen levels and look at the satellite images: we're in the middle of a cyclone!"

In fact, a strange calm had settled outside: neither rain nor wind, it seemed as though time had stopped in its tracks.

"It won't last for very long, then we'll get out of the eye of the cyclone, and then all hell will break loose again. But there's a problem, something strange: the nitrogen levels are changing!"

"Frank, come here: look outside." Rita noticed that it was strangely dark outside and a strange blue light was nearing the center.

"Get out of here, Rita. We have to go downstairs!" said Frank breathlessly, and then grabbed her arm and ran her down to the basement.

"What's happening?" exclaimed Rita, frightened.

"I don't know, but we'd better stay hidden and quiet" said Frank, resolutely, no longer knowing which way to turn.

The research center emergency light went out.

"Strange, could it be a short circuit?" Rita said to Frank.

"No, it's not a short circuit. My laptop computer turned off by itself. So the hurricane has passed and we're in the eye of the storm right now. Outside it's deadly calm, and we saw a blue light nearing the center. Then, it felt strangely hot just before we came back upstairs, and now all the lights have gone out! This must be electromagnetism and that outside must surely be..."

"Must be?" Rita said, curiously.

"Aliens! I don't believe that much in them, but this is how they make themselves known; now I'll show you. Let's hide behind the door of the nitrogen genetic containers; it's made of lead, and as you already know, that type of material won't let radiation pass through it. If my laptop turns back on, it'll mean that we're in the presence of an alien landing that is radiating the center!"

"Let's get out of here….I'm scared silly!" Rita said as Frank held her.

They headed for the door, opened it, went inside, and then closed it. There was no electricity on the internal circuit, but then Frank's laptop turned on.

"Did you see that?" The radiation is blocking us in. Who knows what will happen now. If I put two and two together, it makes me think that they must have approached Earth by taking advantage of the hurricane and then remained hidden by the clouds; now they've gone into the eye of the cyclone, and now they're here above us. But what do they want? Why radiate the center? Oh hell! They're not radiating the center: they're radiating the genetic containers! Dammit!"

"Thank goodness there are only two left and these one here together with the other ones in the other building are protected!" Rita said suddenly.

"There's nothing else for us to do but wait and see!"

After 10 minutes, the emergency light came back on.

"Now we can get out of here, let's go upstairs but be careful," Frank said to Rita.

Together they went upstairs where there was still the same bleakness of broken glass and furnishings on the ground; Rita opened the door to look outside while Frank decided to destroy the two remaining containers, still under nitrogen.

Threatening clouds and rain were making their way back.

"Let's destroy these two containers outside. Rita, help me. Let's go in the other building to decontaminate and destroy the genes!"

They got ready to work: Frank hugged Rita and kissed her tenderly. He had wanted to do it for his entire life: he loved her to death and now was the time to let it show: "I love you Rita," he said, with his heart full of joy. "I love you too Frank," said his beloved, but now there was no more time. Frank took a nitrogen container with his cart and took it to be destroyed, while Rita prepared the other one to be obliterated, but their lives were in the hands of fate.

The hurricane engulfed the center while Frank was leaving the building next door to get a second container.

Winds blowing 280 kilometers per hour and a sheet of rain swallowed Frank up and all the surrounding areas.

"Frank…Frank!" Rita began desperately to scream. "Sweetheart, where are you?"

Sinister fate.

She couldn't go outside to look for him as Rifran was going by outside.

She hid in the basement.

Upstairs she heard the wind, the rain, and…cried.

"Why, Frank, why? I loved you so much…why did our relationship begin so soon but end so fast?"

Rita felt so desperate that she fainted!

The hellish hurricane had taken Hamilton where the research center was and the entire island by storm. The destruction caused by the hurricane lay beneath everyone's eyes: before the treetops caressing the skies, sadly fallen like warriors overcome by war's hatred, road signs and billboards strewn everywhere, security cameras destroyed and vanished into thin air; their car carried away by Rifran's fury and a strange smell in the air.

The smell of death!

Nature getting its revenge!

Finally, the rescuers arrived!

Policemen and firemen reached the area hit by the natural disaster and the research center with their endless rescue vehicles.

Specialized personnel took out the nitrogen containers. Others, on the other hand, stirred the debris to restore the whole area back to its original condition and began searching for any survivors.

The rescuers had quite a bit of trouble getting inside the research center as the sealed door was closed and didn't leave much hope of them getting inside.

It was blasted open!

Rita was found on the floor below unconscious, and the doctor there, ascertaining that she had only fainted, felt it appropriate to admit her to the hospital for further analysis.

In the meantime, the entire area was marked off and the nitrogen containers were put in other genetic centers.

Unknown voices inundated Rita's ears.

She woke up slowly but surely, confused.

"What happened?" she asked the doctor of the hospital ward.

"Don't worry, it's all over. You're here in the hospital because you fainted when the hurricane hit the area. Do you remember?

"Yes, I remember strong gusts of wind and lots of rain and then darkness," Rita said to the doctor.

"The documents show that your name is Rita Minzon and that you're a genetic researcher at the Hamilton Research Center. That's where we found you."

"Yes, that's right, that's where I work, but now I'm all confused."

"I understand, get some rest, we'll see each other later," the doctor said to the patient. And he left.

Rita though again and again, trying to remember something, any little thing that was not coming to her right then and there.

The days passed and the treatment continued. Rita pulled herself together when an ambulance arrived at the emergency room.

Rita realized someone was coming when she heard the siren sounding.

And soon she realized that the person was that very special someone: Frank!

Doctors and nurses ran around, getting ready to tend to the patient in the emergency room.

Once he had been settled, he was taken to Rita's room because she had been released.

She was about to leave when he saw a stretcher carrying a patient in the corridor to her former room.

Curious to know who would be the person to take up her hospital bed, Rita remained speechless, her mouth wide open, and her eyes began to fill with tears.

"Frank! You're not dead! Frank!" she began to yell.

After having explained the situation to the doctors, Rita was given permission to stay to help her little Frank.

"They found him buried in dozens of cubic meters of rubble in the area surrounding the center; now he's sedated and can't hear you. He has a concussion and a fractured arm, but that's all: he was lucky he didn't die. He was hit by a level-four hurricane!" said the doctor to Rita.

"Thanks, doctor, I'm here now, I'll help him, thanks again," Rita said to the doctor.

He left the room.

There, lying on the bed, motionless, one arm wrapped up in a cast and his head bandaged up, the IV slowly letting the seconds pass by with its continuous and uninterrupted dripping.

"Frank, I love you and I'm here next to you, I won't leave you, sweetheart."

Rita sat next to Frank's bed, her hand caressing him tenderly. Every once in a while, with some wet gauze, she would dampen his lips. And she would pray.

Tenderly and lovingly, Rita would often reposition Frank on the bed: sometimes from one side, sometimes from the other, paying attention to adhere to the directions the doctors had given her: a couple of hours on one hip, another two on the other hip, and the same amount of time lying on his back. As soon as she saw him wiping his lips, she would dampen them and check the IV. If she needed any help, the doctors were ready to intervene at any time.

"Ma'am, do you want some coffee?" said the nurse, as she passed by to see how the situation was.

"Yes, thank you, I really need one: I want to stay awake and help my little Frank. Thank you," she answered.

After a little while, she was brought some black coffee with some toasted bread and jam.

By that time, she had stayed for two days with Frank hand in hand, day and night, her eyes watching the IV drops that seemed as though they were tracking the seconds of those dark, sad moments.

Outside, in the meantime, life was slowing getting back to normal in the aftermath of the hurricane. The affected area was being cleared up with great effort, the trees cut into small pieces and stowed away, and the signs were put back up again.

They had to move on.

Emergency crews, meanwhile, had already taken steps to deposit the nitrogen containers in other research centers close by, having to be constantly monitored and placed in clean rooms.

Slowly the white beaches began to come alive again. They never finished working. Day and night, they put back up everything that the hurricane had carried away: stands, beach umbrellas, restaurants, and tourist attractions.

After about a week, the containers from the Hamilton center, were put back into working order in the new research center about thirty kilometers away: one next to the other, in the clean room...all twenty of them.

That's right, twenty!

While working, the emergency crew had even unearthed contaminated containers that they hadn't realized at all had been placed together with the others.

The dilemma was that the tubes with the frozen embryos in them were meant for the so-called "end process," the typical fertilization process.

In the meantime, Rita tried to rest up a bit in an armchair that was kindly given to her by the hospital nurse staff.

She got so lost in her "hit and run" dreams that the doctors' assistants had to take her away to her dear Frank.

After yet another tense nap, Rita got up from the armchair and went to the bathroom to freshen up.

Once she turned off the faucet, the water, which stopped dripping in the sink, seemed like it wanted to mark time passing, like the continuous and hypnotic dripping of Frank's IV.

Now that feeling had become a part of her.

Once she got back to her room, she turned on the TV on low volume for news from the outside world: life began laboriously again.

She sat on the bed and admired her beloved. She planted a kiss, like strong summer thunder, with all her love and might on Frank's forehead.

Was it the kiss, or was it the TV on to shake him out of his unconsciousness? Whatever it was, the fact was that Frank opened his eyes!

"My little Rita," he said in a whisper "sweetheart, where am I ... what happened?"

Bouncing off the bed as if overcome by a mysterious force, Rita called the doctor and said, weeping: "sweetheart, it's me, sweetheart, it's all over ... sweetheart, how are you?"

Meanwhile, the doctors and nurses came in to check on the patient "how is Frank," asked the doctor; "Dazed and confused" Frank replied, who meanwhile had reached out his hand in search of Rita's. Sitting next to him, she continued to cry and thanked the good Lord for answering her prayers.

"Dear, do you remember anything?" she said again;

"Very little, only wind, thunder and rain ... then nothing more," said Frank.

"Now let let him rest," said the doctor: "You need to do the same as well, Miss Minzon."

Rita kissed Frank and left the room; the hospital staff set her up in a room just for her so that she could get some sleep.

And sleep she did: when she woke up, she was brought a meal that would have been enough for three people; she cleaned off her plate, gobbling up all the delicious food that staff nurses had kindly brought to her.

Meanwhile, Frank continued recovering, eating and regaining his strength while he watched the damage Hurricane Rifran had done on the news broadcast.

And he remembered everything!

Shaken up, he got out of bed trembling, and headed for the door.

He opened it and went out into the hall.

"Rita, Rita!" he began to scream.

Doctors and nurses rushed to see what was happening, as did Rita, arriving out of breath: "What is it, sweetheart? What are you doing standing up?" she said.

"The contaminated containers have been found and taken to the research center!" said Frank, alarmed.

"Damn it, now what?" said Rita, worried.

"We have to go now to collect and destroy them" said Frank, who in the meantime, headed for his room to get his clothes.

"Mr. Isolarb can't get out. He's still under observation!" yelled the doctor.

"I have to go, there are still two nitrogen containers with genes contaminated by aliens!" exclaimed Frank, hoping they would let him leave the hospital.

He hoped as much as he could.

The police were called inside. Seeing how confused Frank was, and making him confirm statements he made regarding the alien contamination, they felt it was appropriate to stop him so as to prevent him from hurting himself or others.

Of course, the police did not believe what he said about the aliens.

"No, he's telling the truth," said Rita suddenly, telling them word for word everything that had happened to them at the research center during the hurricane: about the electromagnetism, the inactivated power lines, the heat, the bluish light and Frank's laptop.

"Okay, we'll check it out, but you two stay calm here," the policeman said to Rita.

"You have to destroy the two containers" Frank screamed "make it quick because there could be contaminated implanted embryos, so hurry up!".

The doctors had Frank and Rita sit in the room while the police headed to inspect the research center.

They reached Cross Bay, a village a few kilometers from the research center in Hamilton where the containers had been placed.

The police car stopped in front of the building's front door and the facility manager, bewildered, asked them what they wanted right then and there.

"We've received a report" the policeman said to the researcher "two of your colleagues: researcher Frank Isolarb and Rita Minzon from Hamilton Research Center have told us about two of the contamination containers in your possession; they say that the same has occurred during the Hurricane. Can we check it out? "

"Certainly," said the manager, "Follow me, I'll show you where the containers are, but first, you'll have to clean yourselves off and put on sterile gown and overshoes."

The doctor and the police walked into the research center.

Once they had cleaned themselves off and put on sterile gowns, the doctor and the police entered the room where containers from the Hamilton research center had been placed.

"They're all the same, how do we find the two that the researcher Isolarb claims are contaminated?" said the policeman.

"There's no way of knowing," said the doctor: "As you can see, the containers are all identical and deriving from our data, in the various monitorings, it doesn't look like there are any contaminations or other changes in the parameters of sorts: it's all under control!"

"Okay, we've done our job of checking everything," the policeman said again, "looks like everything is normal." If for any reason you notice changes of any kind, please call us immediately and we'll look into destroying the containers concerned. "

"We'll keep you informed without a doubt!" said the lead policeman.

They left the room and headed toward the research center exit: "Goodbye doctor," said the policeman.

"Goodbye to you and thanks for the warning" answered the doctor, and every one of them headed on his way: the police drove off in the direction of Hamilton hospital while the researcher went back into his office, picked up the phone and called the university to bring them up-to-date on the situation.

"The police came here to the center," he said, "we were told that there are two containers of contaminated genes and if we see the changes in nitrogen or in DNA to warn them immediately to have them destroyed. How should we proceed? "

"Destroy them? Are you out of your mind? Do you know how much two containers cost for the company? A year's worth of salaries wouldn't be enough to pay for even one of them! No, no they can't be destroyed, go on with your work and don't mind the monitoring. They have definitely told you lies!"

After these clear indications were given, he hung up the telephone receiver.

The research center was freed from any responsibility.

At the hospital, meanwhile, Frank and Rita walked nervously up and down the halls.

"We must do something," Frank said to Rita, who in the meantime was sitting in an armchair. "We can't stay here hand in hand."

"What do you think we should do? They won't let us leave, "said Rita.

"The fact that they won't let us leave doesn't mean we can't do it," Frank said, resolutely. "I have a plan in mind, listen: you take some of our things from the room and hide them where you can. Leave the room, go into the bathroom and leave everything rolled up there behind the toilet or the sink then come back here. I'll do the same thing, and ten minutes later, you'll come back to the bathroom too, we'll climb out the window, and once we're outside, we'll take a taxi and go racing to Cross Bay and, once we've arrived, we'll destroy containers! "

"You're crazy, but I'll go along with you anyway. It is the only way to avoid the worst from happening," said Rita standing up from her armchair, ready to take action.

They opened the closet in the room and took everything out that they would need to carry out their plan, then, once they had hidden everything well, they left to put their plan into action.

First it was Rita's turn, then Frank's.

They walked casually along the endless corridors, when, at a certain point, Rita, standing next to the nurse, saw someone leave.

"Is everything all right, Miss Minzon?" said the doctor, leaving the room.

"Just fine, doctor I was ... I was looking for the bathroom, can you tell me where it is?" Rita said, ready to tell a joke.

"Up ahead, the second door on the right," said the doctor.

"Thank you so much" Rita said, hurrying up as if it were physiological urgent need!

She went in the bathroom, closed the door, took off her shirt, and "dumped" the clothes she had around her waist on the floor.

Once she came out, it was Frank's turn to go in.

As soon as Rita went in the room, a quick and clear glance made it clear to Frank that it was time.

Frank came out, went to the bathroom and after ten minutes Rita came to move on to the next phase of the plan: the Escape!

"Nobody saw me: we can go," he said.

They locked the bathroom door, opened the window, and once they tied together the clothes they had hidden, they turned it into a "lucky rope" to drop down three meters that were between the window and the ground below.

"Green light," Frank said to Rita. "Let's go."

They dropped down through the bathroom window and escaped trying not to get an eyeful.

"Taxi!" shouted Frank, pointing to the first taxi he saw.

The taxi approached them, pulled up beside the curb and the two of them got in: "To the genetic research center Cross Bay, make it quick!" Frank said to the driver.

They left.

The taxi sped through the streets of Hamilton fast. "Faster please, faster," Frank said again, "I'll pay any fines you get, but, make it quick!"

The taxi passed cars and overtook them repeatedly. The driver constantly sounded the horn to make his way through traffic.

Frank and Rita held hands while they held the rear door handles with their free hand to avoid banging their heads on the car windows.

Meanwhile, two black vans approached the Cross Bay research center: large and sealed, they had come to pick up the containers then bring to the hospital to insert genes contained in the test tubes.

The final countdown had begun!

"Miss Minzon? Do you hear me, Miss Minzon?" said the doctor from the hospital, knocking repeatedly on the bathroom door.

"Doctor, doctor! Mr. Isolarb is not in his room," said the nurse, running.

"We'll knock down the door, dammit," the doctor said.

The bathroom door was knocked down with two sound kicks: inside there was only a pile of clothes, an open window and not a soul outside.
"

"Call the police, they've escaped!" the doctor said to the nurse.

Security was called in via radio: "Calling all units: two researchers from the research center, Mr. Frank Isolarb and his colleague Rita

Minzon, have escaped from Hamilton hospital. We think they're heading toward the Cross Bay research center. They're not armed. They must be stopped and reported back immediately! ".

The signal was received by the area patrols and also from the one returning to the Cross Bay center.

"Here are two cars, we are in the area. Let's proceed with the checkpoint," he said.

The squad stopped: it closed one lane to allow traffic to slow down and so have more control in the cars passing by.

After fifteen minutes, the policeman saw a taxi approaching at high speed honking to make its way through.

"We're there, they're coming," he said to his colleague who turned on the car ready to chase them.

"Dammit, the police, what do we do?" Rita said to Frank.

"What do you think we should do? If they stop us, they'll block us and then you can say goodbye to your containers. "

The driver knew what he had to do, pushing on the accelerator, "They'll take away my driving license and registration this time, "she thought to herself, and began to zigzag between the cars lined up one behind the other seeing as the road was narrowing.

The policeman put out the signaling disk to bring them to a halt, but that didn't stop them!

The car passed in front of the patrol squad as quick as lightning, which went chasing the taxi, the tires screeching.

The policeman called the station.

"Here is car number two. We're following a taxi heading straight for the Cross Bay research center. Let's ask for reinforcements," said the policeman to those at the station.

"Right away" said the person from the other end. "We're sending units three and five to help. We'll be able to see you in a few minutes!"

The taxi's wheels like the ones of the patrol squad car went whirling like Rifran days ago: the screeching tirs, horn and siren could already be heard far from the Cross Bay Center, where some containers had been loaded in vans.

"The two Hamilton researchers are coming," said the head of the center: "Let's hurry and load up the vans behind the building!"

The taxi continued its mad race, three police cars behind it now, trying in vain to stop it.

"There are two cars here. We are at the road entrance to the research center and would like to intervene...we'll shoot the tires!" the policeman said to the operator, she answered: "If there aren't any other options, go ahead and do it!"

And there were no other options!

The taxi came in, blowing up a great cloud of dust on the white road to the research center, when a gunshot loud like summer thunder blew the rear left side of the car which crashed and spun out of control. It stopped on one side of the road completely surrounded by a dense fog of dust.

Once the cloud of dust had dissolved a few seconds later, he heard: "Everyone stop, the police is here!"

The cloud dissipated and out came the taxi driver, white and frightened, his hands held up: "I surrender, I surrender, take the taxi if you want, but I surrender!"

The police surrounded the car quickly and opened the rear car windows carrying guns in their hands.

The noise from the excavation and that of a few pebbles in their shoes now moved along rhythmically with Frank and Rita, who had already run fast away from the taxi and Police!

They arrived at the center and tried to get in but the sealed door was closed of course.

They walked around the building to see if there were any other windows or doors open.

Everything was closed!

Frank, who knew no more than the devil, walked away from the building's perimeter walls and told Rita his idea.

Both being researchers, they were familiar with the genetic center buildings.

First of all, they knew never get too close to the perimeter walls: the security cameras are always on and then there is always a building next door: like in Hamilton.

They knew that the contaminated containers were in the main building: the vans were parked in the back and Hamilton containers were most definitely the first ones to have disappeared from circulation while they definitely had stored "normal" containers in the building next door.

Frank went in the other building and cut off the electricity, sounding the black-out alarm and hiding himself.

Rita hid behind a van, waiting for the back door to open for her to go into the center.

The Cross Bay manager, imagining a plot hatched by the two researchers, decided to deactivate the alarm using the electrical panel placed outside the back door, without having to go to the building next door, also because of everything Frank imagined there could be!

Too bad Rita was waiting for him at the back door, hidden behind a van parked just in front of the entrance.

Rita came in at the speed of lightening and, even if the camera detected the intrusion, nothing could prevent the armored door from opening from the inside.

Frank came out of his hiding place and went in.

"What are the right containers?" exclaimed Rita

"There is no way of knowing, the only thing left to do is to destroy them all!"

They went into the control room, and quickly began to move the various levers that managed the containers: multi-colored LED started to turn off; Rita left the room to remove the containers from the emergency group generator.

They heard three distinct sounds:

The first was the anti-black-out alarm, the second was the vans leaving and the third...

The laughter of the evil research center manager, who made it known that not all containers had been destroyed!

"What were you planning on doing?" said the person in charge to the police who had arrived in the meantime. "They destroyed the containers and burned so many millions of dollars: arrest them."

The police arrested Frank and Rita. Although now powerless, they tried to explain the threat of imminent danger to the authorities, but it was useless.

The genes had been implanted. Their stupidity and selfishness now prevailed.

Dozens, hundreds of women, pregnant women, were taken to the hospital.

Recurrent nightmares during the long night hours plagued them!

Was it a bad omen?

Frank and Rita's cell, as fate would have it, had a grating that looked out on the hospital:

"Now what will happen?" said Rita to Frank

"I don't know, but I don't think anything good ... like the hurricane!" he replied.

The following night, the two researchers were awakened by a strange wave of heat and a strange aura of silence:

"Here we are, fate has completed its mission," said Frank, rubbing his eyes and going immediately to look at the hospital through the grating:

A bluish light in the darkness of the night had already wrapped itself around the hospital like a bad omen.

Frank hugged Rita, kissed her again, and glanced outside:

"Let's hope the new generation," he said, "will be less stupid than the current one!"

And together, powerless, they closed their eyes.

3. RODOTHAR

Sitting at her desk, with the computer turned on, Mrs. Wign's just didn't feel like doing that bill that should have already been ready by four o'clock.

Her fervent mind distracted her from everything else except concentrating on numbers and VAT percentages!

"Lady Wign's, I'm going out for a couple of hours, I'll let you take care of the appointments." There it was, the only voice she heard that boring day, the voice from the main speaker announcing two hours of complete solitude ... as if that were not already enough.

How bored she was!

She heard the door being closed hastily. Here, she thought, I can finally have a cigarette!

A great sense of emptiness overcame Mrs. Wign's as she bent over to get her bag ... a great sense of emptiness.

She put her purse on the desk: the walnut table perfectly matched that bag, it looked like one thing lumped together; but she didn't pay much attention to this as to the despair she felt in that instant.

She took the pack of cigarettes, lit one, making the inert match slide on the ashtray beside her. "Be brave," cried a medium-low voice and sighing momentarily, she breathed in deeply to fill her lungs with oxygen. Her lungs had now grown accustomed to the microclimate of the office and a few too many cigarettes!

She closed her eyes, how can I be brave ... the computer there in front of her seemed to be waiting for someone to touch the keyboard.

"I really need to give myself a break," she thought, also because the holidays were now a distant memory of the past year, "Yes, I think I'll leave this place!"

The continuous rhythmic noise of the wheels on the rails, the rocking of the carriages cradling her senses, already announced what would be a relaxing and long journey: she had brought cash in her purse ... but not too much: better to avoid problems… a credit card, a suitcase with the handle redone, and a great desire to travel; She had taken one of those bunks with a compartment door always easily slammed along the windy routes, with people walking by talking of this and that, the controller checked her ticket and off she went ... finally Mrs. Wign's was free to go travelling!

Feeling quite satisfied, she opened a book. One of those books that the past sometimes forgets that, once you re-evaluate them, it lets your imagination take you away and make you think about what we once were ... many, many years ago.

The lights came on, the sun was already greeting the day full of commitments. Here ... the classic sound of the train entering a tunnel, lulled by the sound and the usual rocking of the carriages. What an exciting story she was reading, having already read half the book.

"Dad mom?" shouted a girl from the hallway; Mrs. Wign's looked up from the yellowed pages of her book, thought for a while and ... her eyes began to redden and some tears fell down those cheeks often covered by a thin layer of makeup: that voice had brought her back to a time when her parents would travel around the peninsula by train for her father's work…

Mrs. Wign's loved her elderly parents. "Mom?" exclaimed the little girl opening the door of Mrs. Wign's bunk. "No, I'm not your mom, sweetheart, try the door next to this one, "said the girl with a red handkerchief around her neck that made Mrs. Wign's think of a time even farther back in the past.

The little girl waved goodbye and closed the door.

Mrs. Wign's returned her gaze to the pages of her book.

"May I?" asked a young woman opening the compartment door where the bunk was situated, "May I?".

"Of course, come in!" said Mrs. Wign's.

That young woman who had just walked in was spright, dressed elegantly and looking very active. She seemed accustomed to roaming for work or having many hobbies.

A very kind and polite guy just over fifty years old with blonde hair and blue eyes sat in the seat on the metro, looking for a bit out the window.

The road was long, she had finished about a quarter of her book… when Mrs. Wign's asked the woman what she did for a living to dampen the monotonous air that had arisen.

"I'm a nurse!" she said, "I take the train to work, it's more convenient considering all the traffic and the long distance."

They talked about this and that for almost an hour: mostly about work problems. While Mrs. Wign's talked about her terrible monotonous daily life and work routine as a company secretary, the nurse whose name was Mirel shared her experiences with her patients suffering from various diseases ...interesting job thought Mrs. Wign's.

Other topics of discussion were their children, with all their problems for building a future and the various stages of adolescence; taking care of family and elderly parents, problems with various merciless diseases, when you see one of your parents who has always loved and appreciated life, reduced to a state of absolute mental retardation for which they don't even recognize you anymore ... organic diseases that lead you to a life full of obligations ...all because of that!

A tangible wave of sadness invaded the coach.

A curious red bracelet adorned Mirel's wrist. "A simple ribbon but one with an important meaning!" Mirel said:" One of my favorite pastimes was playing with my dog Nile, a beautiful black beagle with brown paws that unfortunately died a little while ago. "A loving tear trickled down her cheek, as if to highlight all the love she felt for her beloved creature Mirel. "I even have a cat: Crumb but two more have already arrived, overall between my cats and my fish in the tub in my beautiful garden, I have my work cut out for me, "she whispered with a loving smile.

Meanwhile, the train sped fast into the dark areas of the peninsula when Mirel stood up, took Mrs. Wign's hand and looking her straight in the eyes greeted her because the next stop would be hers. With a gentle but energetic handshake, Mirel said goodbye to Mrs. Wign's saying, "Goodbye, although we will be far away from each other, we will always be here, together, to observe the landscape pass by out the window!" She left, closing the door behind her.

Mrs. Wign's was very struck by Mirel's words... what did they mean?

To forget about it, she took her old book, but the late hour had got the best of her. So she decided to pull down the "bed", close the door and sleep a bit.

She fell asleep right away; perhaps because the day had been long or perhaps it was the rocking of the carriage and the rhythmic sound of the wheels on tracks that were making her sleepy, the fact is that Mrs. Wign's sank into a slumber that she had wanted to do for quite a long time!

Voices of people in the compartments next to Mrs. Wign's did not in the least disturb her as she now lied abandoned in Morpheus' arms like a baby in those of his mother.

The train sped fast into the night; every once in while they would go into a tunnel, every once in a while they would have a railroad switch.

Finally dawn came. The dawn of a new day!

Happy and relaxed, Mrs. Wign's woke up, getting out of the bed suspended in "mid-air" and she walked sleepily to the bathroom to freshen up.

There was no line. "I'm lucky!" she thought.

After washing up as she would normally do, she sat down in the compartment, waiting for breakfast to be served; the trees darted fast in front of the window, so fast that they seemed like a light impressionistic-style painting!

"Excuse me, ma'am? Breakfast is served" said the train attendant, a tall, thin man, wearing a blue jacket and trouser, and a moustache that vaguely reminded her of distant relatives.

Mrs. Wign's stood up uneasily, walked to the dining car, where above tables clearly from the nineteenth century, made a fine display, a myriad of colorful fresh fruits, sweets and jams, with teapots steaming hot filled with English tea and even milk, coffee, juices ... everything that a traveler who has just woken up could ever want in the morning.

Mrs. Wign's sat down at a table where the girl with the red handkerchief around her neck from the night before was waiting.

"Did you find your mother?" said Mrs. Wign's to the little girl, "It is, it's that lady who is picking some fruit!" replied the child.

The child's mother arrived with a tray of fruit and jams, a little bit of milk and tea and sat down next to her daughter facing Mrs. Wign's. After just a couple of minutes, the little girl's father came up to the table.

"Good morning ma'am," said the child's mother to Mrs. Wign's. "Excuse my daughter for yesterday evening ... you know, she went into the wrong compartment!" "Don't worry about it," said Mrs. Wign's. "It was absolutely a pleasure to see such a pretty little creature."

There was something familiar about those eyes, that family that she had never seen before ... so familiar, so strange.

Breakfast lasted about twenty minutes, and after, the family politely said goodbye to Mrs. Wign's, going back to their compartment.

"I have a book waiting to be read," Mrs. Wign's thought to herself.

She got up and walked toward her compartment. She opened the door and went in...as if she were at home ... her home. This solo trip was bringing something new to her life, something exciting, something "déjà vu" that made her feel something deep within her.

Then all those people ... the girl with the red handkerchief, her mother and her father ... so close, and yet ...and that nurse with the red bracelet with her love for animals ... just like Mrs. Wign's.

How strange.

The book was now nearing its end, but this did not matter to Mrs. Wign's.

It was an old book forgotten in the cellar, full of dust and pages yellowed with age, but this did not matter to Mrs. Wign's; she had read and re-read it many times, and the book still gave her the same good feeling....a great read..

Surely this time, having just read the last page, she would have begun to read it again, so she could relive old feelings.

The train stopped at the station, some people got off, some got on. Slowly the trees began to chase one another again, when, all of a sudden, a distinct man much younger than Mrs. Wign's with a baby in his arms knocked on the door: "Can I come in?" he said in a gentleman-like manner. "Please come in," said Mrs. Wign's.

She did not pay much attention to the new guest. She was so immersed in her book; she only had a few pages left to read and would do anything to live once again the ending so exciting that so often made her cry!

Another tunnel ... sometimes tunnels can be seen as dark moments in one's life ... after the light of day comes the darkness of night... the positive and the negative ... the good and the bad.

These were her thoughts. It must have been the darkness that made Mrs. Wign's doze off for a bit.

Or at least that's what she thought.

When she woke up, she looked around ... she was alone in the compartment; on the man's seat, there was a frame ... a frame holding a ticket.

She went out into the hall: the man with the child had disappeared into thin air; the family she had just had breakfast with that morning... was gone.

They must've got off the train at the previous stop while Mrs. Wign's slept.

In life everyone has their stops.

Mrs. Wign's returned to her compartment, disappointed for not having had the chance to say goodbye to the travelers. "Too bad!" she murmured.

She sat down again in her seat, glanced at that so common frame and the ticket.

The frame was the size of a normal photograph, a silver frame finely decorated in relief with floral ornaments; not able to help herself, Mrs. Wign's took it, looked around for a moment, sat down again in her seat, and pulled out the ticket from inside the frame.

The note said: "You're still so beautiful ... a gem shinier than a star! Thanks for everything ... now and forever. "

This trip had a meaning at this point, but what was it?

He thought that there had to be a connection between the little girl, her parents; a link on well Mirel, the nurse and the gentleman with the child. But which one was it?

Disoriented, she took her beloved handbag, something very precious to her. Her mother had given it to her as a gift many years before, but it was still sturdy and spacious. She opened it, put the book inside, and put on a bit of makeup, just to hide the most conspicuous of wrinkles on her face.

Meanwhile, the surrounding countryside, with its glades and natural beauties, were outlined by the train passing fast as the wind.

The controller passed by again: "Is everything okay?" he exclaimed. "All's fine, thanks," said Mrs. Wign's, the events of the long trip still surprising and intriguing her.

"Please ma'am, come" the controller said to a traveler.

"May I come in?" the traveler asked.

"Yes, please do" said Mrs. Wign's again; it seemed as if she were in the back of the office where she worked, constantly seeing so many people!

"Pleased to meet you, I'm Lady Mary," said the lady. A flashy, but friendly character.

"I'm Mrs. Wign's. Nice to meet you," she said, getting up from her seat to shake the lady's hand.

"Have you been traveling for a long time? I'm going down to Geneva," said the showy lady.

"Yes," replied Mrs. Wign's. "Since last night. I'm going to Rodothàr on vacation."

"Rodothàr? Never heard of that place! Is it very far?"

"Yes, very" replied Mrs. Wign's. "It's one of those places where we'll all end up sooner or later, one of those places that let's say ... you cannot do without visiting them! And there are endless blue skies over fresh, green meadows, where you feel like lying down on the ground even with the roar of the falls along with you in that relaxing moment when ... " Mrs. Wign's was interrupted by the hostess telling them that lunch was being served in the dining car.

"Is it already lunch time? Damn how fast time flies, just like this train, fast and sure of its tracks!" said Mrs. Wign's, the expression on her face a cross between amazed and hungry!

Mrs. Wign's, along with the new traveler, Lady Mary, stood up and together they went to the dining car.

The very table in the dining car where she had had breakfast with the little girl's family was there, just as it had been that morning, set and ready again to welcome new guests; they decided to sit right there, facing each other.

Various discussions were underway in the background about countless local delicacies (the kitchen prepared meals based on the places they travelled through!); there were always new tidbits, new flavors like the rest of life.

As always after a sumptuous banquet, a little bit of relaxation is always necessary to letyour food digest!

A trip ... an experience always ready to bring new, endless surprises.

As endless as the train, which goes right, safe and fast in its endless tracks.

Mrs. Wign's began to think, her mind wandering off to who knows where; Lady Mary certainly would never have dared to disturb her while Mrs. Wign's was transported away, both body and soul, her eyes closed and her head leaning against the window, recalling memories ... of her life!

She looked so peaceful. Ecstatic.

Even the train was running strong ... as much as Mrs. Wign's heart. She often wondered why a feeling so strong and new but at the same time so ... familiar. Déjà vu!

"And 'it's time to" rang out loud like thunder, Lady Mary's voice.

"Yeah, that's right" said Mrs. Wign's "it's time to" and without saying another word, they stood up and went to spend another minute of their lives to taste the steaming drink prepared with accurate wisdom by the kitchen workers.

The steam rose as high as the train's, more or less dense but still free flowing, planning to fly high way up there, where it's possible to see the world without anything blocking the view, this life ...travel freely with the slightest breath of wind ... running strong, mingling with other puffs of steam, with another twenty as a whole ... to feel so united in peace and harmony. We have no such luck: wars spurred by perpetrators; abandoned childhoods; poverty, hunger, racism. Everyone thinks only about themselves; altruism is a rare thing!

A child left alone in the middle of a dark, sad and lonely alley, his hand held out in search of a coin for a piece of bread ... not to mention those who take advantage of such situations to make judgements on the others' misfortunes.

Young soldiers sent to die in a country far from their own ... with their loved ones and friends far away ... unfortunately only the memory of their support ... but this is the same old story;

firefighters who die in the rubble;

a wife and a son who await the return of her husband and his father from work but who will not come back;

oil wells on fire for ... again it's the same old story!

A daughter disowned for marrying to a black man ... and then we all are supposed to be united as one? Racism doesn't exist? Why?

If love is love ...

By now her tea had become warm.

It seems impossible that the smoke coming from her cup of tea could carry her mind so far away.

But that's life.

Unfortunately.

Lady Mary had already served herself... the empty cup gave off some tiny specks of dust in the ... seemed to see Mrs. Wign's and other travelers that train immersed in the cosmic universe!

Rodothàr was drawing ever so closer but still ever so far away...

They were getting ready for dinner: the waiters were setting tables and chairs for what would be the last meal of the day.

The old finely-finished tables were decorated with elegant lace tablecloths that fell gently from the sides of the tables themselves, and the folds of precious fabrics looked like they were caressing the table edges themselves.

Refined, decorated china dishes, glasses and shiny sparkling crystal, silver cutlery waiting to be matched up, to be used, a bouquet of flowers and a candle on the refinished table as if it were a work of art.

And perhaps it was.

Time flew by, perhaps because she had spent it finishing reading the last quarter of her book ... Miss Wign's knew the ending by heart... but it was so exciting and beautiful, that every time she read it, it would make her dream all over again.

"... And they lived happily ever after!" As beautiful fairytales sometimes end...fairy tales Miss Wign had always told his son;

"... That long kiss under the sun at dusk just showed how deep their love was for each other!" That's how that romantic and dispassionate novel ended, a novel that had made Miss Wign's dream so much. Maybe because she liked love stories with happy endings or more likely because they resembled her own life story: her life with her husband, Mark!

It was just a kiss at sunset.

They were in the high mountains, years and years ago, she on paid vacation while he was away for work. A meeting, a sinking heart of strong emotions, looks ...those looks that always have remained within them.

Then in the evening or better ... at sunset.

They were in one of those valleys high in the mountains where they left their hearts once they'd admired them.

After a few kilometers of groomed trails on a snowmobile, they ended up on a snow-covered valley surrounded by mountains there since the beginning of time; only the two of them against a backdrop of the sweet pink sunset on the snow ... how peaceful it all was…how high up they were…and then how they kissed!

It was love at first sight.

Those two souls embracing in the midst of the looming heights, then how wonderful their relationship would come to be!

That's precisely how Mrs. Wign's book ended.

And she shed a tear every time she read it.

It was already dinner time.

Talking again about this and that, Mrs. Wign's and Lady Mary walked once again to the dining car: dinner was being served.

Everything was in its place: that same table where the little girl with the red handkerchief and her parents sat, then Mirel and now Lady Mary ... the candlelight reflected off the gleaming crystal glasses.

They were getting closer to Geneva.

The dinner, showcasing several courses of Swiss delicacies, ended about an hour later; they exchanged some words, maybe a joke just to dampen that too aristocratic air to which Mrs. Wign's was not so accustomed.

"It's 'time to lie down" exclaimed Lady Mary, sleepy more from boredom than from fatigue.

"You're right, it's time for me to do the same" said Mrs Wign's, getting up from her chair and heading to their compartment.

Railroad switches and galleries were now a sweet habit: they lulled and relaxed them into the night. Every so often, the sound of the bells at the crossroads ... a few steps down the long corridor of the train ... some items and stops.

So many stops!

Then as if nothing had happened, the train resumed its course ... with more railroad switches and tunnels. ..

Geneva presented itself in its entire splendor the next morning: people down the other that came up, streets and houses unusual compared to those which had used to seeing Mrs. Wign's.

"Goodbye Mrs. Wign's" announced Lady Mary reaching out to shake her hand, "it was a pleasure travelling with you. Thanks for the company!"

"My pleasure," Mrs. Wign's replied "thanks for the company!"

The last gesture Lady Mary made was a long handshake before getting off of the train to disappear then through the streets of this majestic city.

The train whistle sounded ... the train was departing.

Mrs. Wign's settled comfortably at the table in the dining car: the candles burned next to the colorful flower arrangements.

"Ma'am, do you need anything?" said the train attendant suddenly. "Is everything alright?"

"Yes, everything's alright, thanks. There are just two things I want to know: if I can smoke here and how much longer it will take to get to Rodothàr ".

"This is the smoking compartment so you can certainly smoke here, as for Rodothàr ... it is still quite a bit away!" said the man, who after bowing, left through the car door and disappeared into thin air.

Puzzled, Mrs. Wign's opened her purse: there were cigarettes next to her book. She took one and lit it, settling even more comfortably into her seat and resting her elbows on the table.

She took a puff and then looked up, staring at the smoke running after the steaming tea, all the memories from the afternoon spent with Lady Mary.

"Go, run away," said the cigarette smoke: "get off this train and run free like the little girl with the red handkerchief and her parents, the young man with the child in his arms, Mirel remembering Nile and Lady Mary.

And now your time has come, you've reached your stop: get out! Always take the memories from this trip along with you, your life which, though short, it meant everything to you. Rodothàr is still far away, but I'll see it myself ... and I'll find everyone who has traveled with me and got off this train: the little girl who asked me to forgive her for looking for her mom in the wrong compartment…Mirel with her experiences with sick patients ... lady Mary who will be waiting to have a peaceful chat with me with a steaming cup of tea... and the man, the man with the son ... the silver frame! They'll all be there waiting for me. I know it! ".

A strong wave of heat drew closer to Mrs. Wign's fingers: "Ahh!" she shouted loudly!

She opened her eyes...

The PC was there in front of her with, the monitor with the background of her husband and her son who died years ago; the cigarette making a long trail of ashes had burned Mrs. Wign's fingers!

"What happened?" she thought to herself, "it was all a dream!"

She looked over the desk: her beloved purse was there on top of it, open with a novel inside.

Mrs. Wign's wanted a handkerchief. She took her bag but it fell to the ground because her fingers were burnt. Everything inside it fell out.

She reached down to pick it up ... and the volume ... that volume is a book ... or not: it was her personal diary.

She opened it to describe that experience she had just had. She sat comfortably and ... good heavens!

Next to the monitor there was a silver frame engraved with floral patterns ... ... it was a picture of her husband and son and the ticket! In her diary there was a red ribbon which was being used as a bookmark

... a piece of a handkerchief! Speechless and touched, Mrs. Wign's read that page:

"Just us, alone in front of this rosy sunset on the snow ... so peaceful. What a kiss. Love at first sight ... our souls embraced in this valley ... among these eternal heights as eternal as our love. Few stars in the sky because ... you're so beautiful ... you're a light brighter than a star! Thanks for everything ...now and always. I love you. Yours, Mark."

Mrs. Wign's closed the diary, placed it on the desk ... she laid her face on her hand and cried.

After a few minutes, she settled down, feeling something cold touch her hand, and looked up and saw the framed photo of her husband and son above her hand as if to console her with a sweet touch.

"Yes, my sweethearts," she said "as forever eternal as those hills!"

4. THOUGHTS AND WORDS:

Alone?
Life leads you to make hasty decisions: why make such decisions
that could change your life in such short a time?
What can be done, which fork to take: right or left?
You feel so alone!
Then, a voice: "Don't worry ... whatever happens I'm here!"
It then decided, courageously,
to believe in luck!
But with a heart full of joy because, it's just ...
No:
I don't think so!

I, a solitary flower.

A heart as warm as the sun,
two stars for eyes,
a quarter moon, his smile,
his love: rain.
and I...
all alone
like a flower in a field of wheat,
I look up there at infinity!
Hope,
a drop of rain falling on me,
making me grow and grow again,
until, one day, I too
a solitary flower,
can get up there, to be caught by a passing comet ...
thus entering your infinite world.

A blue sea:

There is always a sea beyond the beach
but not everyone sees it.
There are always a lot of things to do
it is a luxury to die!
Turn off the TV
leave that door
let your hair be caressed by the wind
with a heart full of love and joy
walk tall
let the wind come into your lungs
intoxicating energy!
There is always a sea beneath you
a sea of friendship and opportunity
and if a problem makes you sad and lonely
entrust him quietly to a poet ...
as he'll make a light-hearted poem of it.
Then you'll shout at everyone
and everyone will applaud
remembering you
remembering to walk tall
remembering to love!

There outside is a sea
so look with a heart full of hope
reaching out to those who need you too.
Then you'll see beyond the beach,
a blue sea
like the sky,
and as your eyes well up, you thank them!

5.   A DINOSAUR IN SIENA

"All of a sudden, it feels freezing cold.

I open my eyes: where are they?

All round me green and lush forests; I sit up, a bit clumsily ...I haven't seen the world for centuries.

Fear.

I remember a great light and a bang so enormous ... that ...then darkness.

Food supply had already become a problem: the continents had split and had formed Asia, the Americas and Europe was breaking away from Africa.

This led to big problems for wildlife and we began to warn everyone about these "food" issues.

Sorry ... for expressing this feeling of mine:

I'm a Dinosaur: actually, just one of those that seems to have survived from cataclysm of millions of years ago.

To be precise, I'm a Stegosaurus (don't worry, I'm not carnivorous!). I'm considered to be a gentle herbivore, simply put. Stegosauria herbivorous were elephants that populated the world during the Jurassic Period, from 210 million to 144 million years ago, along with ferocious predators like the Allosaurus. Reaching twenty feet from nose to tip of tail, the most recognized stegosaurus, Stegosaurus stenops, had a double row of scales along its back with two or three pairs of spikes on its tail. Other stegosaurs had smaller plates, with bony outgrowths of the skin.

We were 7.8 meters long with dorsal plates that served as ... your solar panels!

Here I am.

I do not know where I am, but now, I can get on my feet.

If you happen to notice me, don't be afraid. I'm a quiet type of guy!

You may think you were back on the set of Jurassic Park; you're only at home. The problem is that I'm not in mine!

I think I'll get out of these green trees to see where I am. I walk around and I seem to see the open spaces there.

I go on.

In front of me, other animals, seeing me, they flee in terror: and now we're getting off to a good start!

I think they're deer and wild boar, but I'm not familiar with this species.

Finally a little bit of air. Finally I'm out of the woods.

I can't believe my eyes and my nose!

Sure, you humans are really asking for it!

Your holes are not made of brushwood and even in caves: concrete buildings!

Excuse me, but isn't it a waste of time to go digging for the foundations and the continuous cast concrete, making sure to leave space for doors and windows?

We live outside in the fresh air which is also healthier!

And what is that smell in the air? What are you up to?

You get around with cars that not only pollute, but they also make you lose your natural ability to "walk".

This makes me angry: you know that cars are fueled with gas and that this same thing comes from oil?

And do you know how many relatives and friends of mine are dissolved in the oil itself?

You have no idea!

When I pass a car, I feel like I can see one of my old ancestors escape from the tailpipe, greet me and disappear in the sky.

This is bad!

I walk around, I leave the woods and I move furtively: I don't want you to see me so that I won't scare you.

I don't know how you'll react!

I've decided I'll move around at night.

I'm a fraction now, I've left the green trees and path where, during the day, everyone heads for the city!

So that way I see new things.

I pass by a dark street; the sign says: "*strada del ferratore*". Who knows what it means.

I walk a bit more and after a while, I come to a clearing; I try to talk to the wind ... you never know ... some of my fellow travelers could possibly hear!

I hear nothing. I'm alone.

I don't let sadness get the best of me. We dinosaurs are determined and strong,

so it's time to go off to the city.

You take good care of yourselves anyway. You're not short of modern commodities: houses with gardens, bars and various shops, places to go shopping, public transport to avoid walking, banks, bakeries.

I also saw one of our cemeteries: the gas station!

I climb up the hill and after I go down it ... look at what I see over there!

Something wonderful!

The shadow of the city, a tower, a cathedral.

I can't wait to get there.

Taking hurried steps, I head to the city through small villages and with each step I take, I'm stunned!

My goodness! This must be the train station; I would have never imagined it like this. I see a tree-lined street, I walk across and reach the top.

Wow, a pharmacy! If it existed in my day, maybe my partner would still be here with me to keep me company."

I wipe my huge eyes and continue on my journey.

La lizza," I see written on the wall. I see those shops, those buses.

On earth I find a brochure. Hooray, the city guide!

How beautiful.

Now I know where I am, what the name of this wonderful place is.

I take the guide and read it: Siena.

I'm in Siena! The city known for the *Palio,* the annual medieval horse race, and its many museums; the city, declared a Unesco site, is filled with art and heritage!

What better place is there to be to open my eyes?

And as a tourist in pursuit of new emotions and memories to take home, I'll start from the very beginning:

Siena is in the middle of a vast landscape of hills, between the valleys of many rivers: Arbia in the south, Merse in the southwest and Elsa in the north, between the hills of Chianti in the northeast, Montagnola to the westand the Crete Senesi to the southeast.

"The mound reminds me of something ... well, let's continue reading".

The actual population is 59,785 in the 2001 General Census population ...

"2001? 2001 How! Oh, how long did I sleep?"

While residents total 52,625, there are people living within the municipality such as those not counted in the census or non- residents who are present. This is presumably due to many students coming from other Italian cities and from abroad staying in the city, but also to the many employees of some large companies (such as Monte dei Paschi bank or the Hospital) that are based out of Siena.

Siena was founded as a Roman colony during the era of Emperor Augustus whose name was Saena Julia.

The few reliable sources available which preceded the settlement talk about the existence of an Etruscan community where the Roman military colony was settled during Augustus' era.

The first document we have which mentions the Sienese community dates back to 70 AD and has Tacitus' signature. In the fourth book of the Histories, the following incident is documented: Senator Manlio Patruito reported to Rome where he was beaten and ridiculed with a mock funeral during his official visit to see Saena Julia, a small military colony of Tuscia. The Roman Senate decided to punish the main guilty ones and to strictly ask the Sienese to have a greater respect for authority.

We do not have documents from the High Middle Ages that can shed light on cases of Sienese civilian life. Is there any news on the establishment of the bishop and the diocese, especially for the dispute between the Bishop of Siena and Arezzo, because of the boundaries of the judicial area of each one: the Lombard king Liutprando intervened in this dispute, pronouncing judgment in favor of the diocese of Arezzo. But the Sienese were not satisfied, and so in 853, when Italy passed from the Lombard dominion to that of the Franks, they managed to obtain the annulment of Liutprando's sentence. It seems, therefore, that during the dominion of the Lombards, Siena was governed by a Gastaldo, a representative of the king: a steward who was later replaced by an imperial count after Carlo Magno's coronation. The first account of which we have concrete news was of Winigi Ranieri's son in 867. After 900 the emperor Ludovico III reigned in Siena. His reign did not last that long because the chronicles detail that the counts returned to power under the new government of King Berengario in 903. In the tenth century, Siena was at the center of important trade routes that led to Rome and, thanks to this, it became an important medieval city. In the twelfth century the city was equipped with communal and consular regulations to expand its territory and its first alliances. This relevant economic and political situation led Siena to fight for northern possessions in Tuscany against Florence. From the first half of the twelfth

century, Siena prospered and became an important commercial center, maintaining good relations with the State of the Church; the Sienese bankers were a reference point for Roman authorities, to whom they asked for loans or financing.

Supporting the Ghibelline cause, Siena found itself again against Florence at the end of the twelfth century, which at the beginning was losing. The Sienese then lost the war at the Battle of Colle Val d'Elsa, which led to the rise of the Government of the Nine in 1287. Under this new government, Siena reached both its economic and cultural peak. After

the plague of 1348, the Sienese Republic began its slow decline, which reached its climax in 1555, when the city had to surrender to Florentine supremacy.

A curious episode, halfway between history and science, happened in southeast

Siena on June 16, 1794, when a meteor hit the city.

The appearance of a big dark cloud emitting smoke, lightning flashes and unusually red lenses forewarned the falling meteorites. The meteorite hit the southeastern part of the city, causing a shower of stones weighing between a few milligrams and three kilograms. There were many eyewitnesses, including some English visitors, so that the falling stones could not be denied by authorities. Because of this, many college students from Italian universities went to Siena to study the phenomenon, question witnesses and make hypothesis on its origins.

Only eighteen hours before the event, Mount Vesuvius had begun to erupt.

This divided scholars into two factions: those who believed that the two events were

connected, despite the volcano being about 450 kilometers southeast of Siena, and

those who believed that the two events were not related and intended to investigate

other leads. It should be considered that, at the height of the Enlightenment, the possibility that stones came down from the sky had been considered a popular belief unable to be explained through rational thinking. This proven and undeniable event, however,

reopened it to continuous debate .

"Interesting ... but don't talk to me about meteorites please, come on over."

It's all so curious. I'll go inside the city mansion. "I'll have to watch where I put my feet ... I would not want to spoil the unique artworks of this city, "I said to myself.

"And for once, I want to allow myself the human luxury of passing by the main street (they call it *il Corso*) and take at least a couple of laps ot it! (how nice, I'm learning Sienese terms,) to feel a part of them and this culture."

I reach the end of the street ... and I do not believe my eyes!

And here is where the horses run in the Palio: Piazza del Campo!

I'm speechless, admiring the immense wonder of this artist's painting in front of me, I read:

"In Piazza del Campo / grows verbena

long live our Siena / long live our Siena

in Piazza del Campo / grows verbena

long live our Siena / the most beautiful city of all cities! »

"And I really believe it!

I can't take my eyes off the facade of the town and the adjoining chapel!

You humans are strange: either you create unique wonders or you destroy the planet!

Well, whoever understands you must be really good!

I want to know everything about Piazza del Campo. "I read:

The space that was to become the square was was a piece of terrain hardened to allow rainwater to flow on it at the beginning of Siena's history. The city center which was still developing was in the northern part of the city, in the *Castelvecchio* area and the future "Campo" was a marketplace, lateral to the main communication roads that passed through the city and located exactly on a crossroads. Here today we can still see the direction arrow for Rome to the southeast, the sea to the south-west and Florence to the north.

The history of the square is strongly interwoven with the construction of the

Town Hall or the Public Palace, which overlooks the square.

The first document that describes how the design of the "Campo" square was planned is from 1169 and refers to the entire valley including both the current square and

Market Square, nowadays behind the Town Hall. That year, the Siena community bought the land that stretched from the current *Logge della Mercanzia* to the current Market Square.

The first mention of a division of the two squares was in 1193 and was concluded that in the meantime at least one partition wall had been built, perhaps to stem rainwater.

Until 1270, with the Twenty-Four Government of (1236-1270), the space dedicated to the

future square was used for fairs and markets.

While, on one hand, the square is not merely a "field", on the other hand, it is not designed "on a drawing board". Although it had not yet taken the shape you can see today, it seems that they had already intended to make a space for both public festivals, analogous to what the Cathedral is for religious parties, both to markets and trade in general.

Once this government was overthrown by the Sienese aristocrats, the Government of Nine (1287-1355) began to think of a "neutral" place for the city government. The Town Hall, which served as the town nucleus, would also be the impetus to allow for consonant accommodation of the square outside.

Paving of the square began in 1327 and ended in 1349. Even today, the central part is paved in a similar way, divided into nine segments commemorating the Government of the Nine.

The skyline and structure of Piazza del Campo did not come about "spontaneously". During the years of its construction, the government of Siena gradually passed laws to standardize facades, space, architectural facades and align the profile and the perimeter of the space. Also important is the the destruction of the church of Saints Peter and Paul (located between the existing lanes of St. Peter and St. Paul), because it was protruding compared to the perimeter of the slowly-defining surrounding buildings."

"I'm speechless. It's unimaginable that you humans have created all that.

Many will have this wrong but instead really ... congratulations!

Now I want to know everything about the town hall and its tower."

It is the palace built by the government of the Republic of Siena between 1298 and 1310 as the seat of Government of the Nine. Stone was not used, but brick was, while the white elements are white marble. Each window is decorated with a nose cone that is contained inside it. The blackbirds are Guelph-like.

The coat of arms of Siena is called the "*balzana*". It is a shield divided into two horizontal portions: the upper one is white, the bottom one black. According to legend, it was meant to symbolize the black and white smoke emerging from the pyre wishes that the legendary founders of the city, Aschio and Senio, sons of Remo, would have lit to thank the gods after the city of Siena was founded.

For their alleged fiery character who, they say, borders on insanity too, Sienese are often called "*balzani*".

The Public Palace of Siena stands tall in Piazza del Campo and is adjacent to the lithe Torre del Mangia.

The two side wings were raised subsequently, which have a longitudinal structure. Each window is decorated with a nose cone that contains it. The holes present on the whole structure once served for the beams to make walkways outside.

The history of the town hall of Siena is very much linked to the design of the Piazza del Campo, where the former is located.

In the years after 1193, the year when there was news of Piazza del Campo being subdivided from another open space, which would become the Market Square, where now

it's located. The Town Hall was built "Bolgano," brand-new in Republic of Siena, and the customs building. It remains, then, that the building is strongly linked to Gothic art and this can be seen from its architecture. The Piazza has been attributed not only as similar to a shell but also to a fan, in fact, speaking of this similarity, if we say that the square was equal to a shell, the white parts of the square are similar to the veining; if, on the other hand, we say that the square in question would be similar to a fan, the white strips would be similar to the sticks of a fan.

Long ago, there was the war between Persians and Florence and it is said that however, they asked the Virgin Mary for help and then the battle ended with his winnings. It is said that the square is also similar to the Madonna's open veil who protected and still protects the city. The materials then that were used for this city are: brick and white stone; and the bricks were put in the shape of chink of fish. The same thing was used for

the church: downstairs, materials such as stone were used and in the upper part materials like brick were employed; and this also gives us a pictorial sense. There are stone arches that are typical of Siena.

Upstairs there are *trifore* (3 windows stringed together). On top of the building the public can see merlons. Finally there is the high tower but only in the lower part can we find marble, and in the top part, stone. The latter is similar to Palazzo Vecchio in Florence.

Until 1270, with the Government of Twenty-Four, the city government was located in the curia of the Church of San Pellegrino. The Council of the Bell, comprised of nobles, was given this name because they would congregrate at the sound of the bell atopt the Mignanelli family's tower (currently located at Banchi di Sopra 15) and had three specific churches as their main meeting places and their offices in the nobles' buildings.

Once this government was overthrown by Sienese aristocrats, replaced by the government of the Nine, they began to think of a "neutral" place for the city government. In 1284 news spread of a new building, which would become the Town Hall. Once the Government of the Nine rose to power in 1287, the final push was made to allow the building to be constructed. While the Bolgano palace was facing what is now Market Square, the Town Hall overlooks Piazza del Campo. But the two buildings stand next to each other.

After nearly two decades of uncertainty, a decision was made to incorporate in the new building the Bolgano and the customs building in 1288. The central body, not very different from today, would be completed between 1300 and 1305. In 1310 the whole building had to be completed for the government of the Nine to move in there in that year.

There are still some interesting facts regarding the timing of the construction of the town hall:

* Not sure if the top floor of the central body of the building (the one with pointed mullioned windows) is contemporary with the first construction or was instead built in 1326, as some historians claim;

* The second floor of the two wings was built only in 1680 but retains its original style and balance the mass of the surrounding buildings; We think, however, that this change in Sienese Gothic style has been performed at the height of the Baroque period.

The Town Hall is still the seat of the modern municipal administration and houses the Mayor's offices, some municipal offices and halls representation. At first floor there is the Civic Museum and the City Theatre Rinnovati. On the second floor is the hall of the City Council and the loggia looking toward the back of the building itself, in the south.

The wide facade of the building reflect the multiple construction periods of: the first fine order of three lights was used the stone, then the brick. The windows, in typical style Siena have three Gothic arches supported on columns side by side, while the the center of each ring of arches and pointed arch main each window, has been added to a coat of arms of Siena.

The central body is raised to a plane with regard to the two lateral wings. On top is a Guelph battlement, ie without the dovetail ends. At the center of the facade a large white disc presents the monogram of Christ. Small holes that underpin the façade are so-called scaffolding holes, where the medieval builders would insert wooden poles to support the necessary scaffolding for the construction site.

The various rooms were used by many magistrates who administered the city for centuries. It now houses the Museo Civico and the Siena's council. In the body of the left, next to the Tower Mangia, is the so-called Courtyard of the mayor, decorated by ancient coats of arms, which is also the entrance to the palace.

The Museum houses numerous masterpieces of Sienese art, frescoes, paintings and sculptures.

The largest room and most famous is that of the Globe, that preserves two masterpieces by Simone Martini: Guidoriccio da Fogliano at the siege of Montemassi and Majesty; Old woman and Sodoma complete the decoration of the frescoes hall.

Adjacent is the Hall of Peace, where Ambrogio Lorenzetti frescoed the very famous scene of the Effects of Good Government and Bad Government (1337-1339): though partially damaged (especially in on the wall of the Bad Government), representing an extraordinary example of political allegory without earlier, with extensive representation of the landscape.

Other important works in the museum are: the marble portal by Bernardo Rossellini (1448), the wooden choir by Domenico di Niccolò (1425-1436), the original panels of the Fonte Gaia by Jacopo della Quercia, frescoes by Spinello Aretino, Domenico Beccafumi, the Italian Unification Hall, with vivid frescoes and sculptures by Giovanni Dupré.

"Wonderful. But what about the tower? This beautiful work of art that can be admired from up above all of this magnificence?"

The Torre del Mangia is located in Piazza del Campo in Siena and was the Town Hall's laic "*Campanile*".

It is named after the nickname,"*mangiaguadagni*," (profit eater) given to its first keeper Giovanni Balducci (or "Duccio"), famous for truly appreciating the pleasures of food enjoyed then squandered his earnings at the dinner table. It is among the highest ancient Italian towers, reaching 102 meters to the lightning rod (depending only to Torrazzo of Cremona).

It was built between 1325 and 1348. According to the chronicles some auspicious coins were buried in its foundations and under every corner ("canto") stones are inserted with Hebrew and Latin letters because "neither thunder nor storm" there could hit there.This practice was very common in the Middle Ages. In addition, the four corners are perfectly oriented in the direction N-S and E-O.

Brothers Francis and Arezzo Muccio (or Minuccio) Rinaldo (1338-40), were given the task of constructing the main building perhaps under the direction of Maestro John Augustine, who was paid as a "worker" in 1339. I of Rinaldo probably built the brick and masonry while part Agostino di Giovanni would have made the top travertine White, designed by the painter Master Lippo, likely Lippo Memmi, in-law of Simone Martini.

The clock was built in 1360 by Bartolomeo Guidi. In 1428 the dial was painted and in 1776 was rebuilt in stone and adorned with a fresco covering a shed. These last two items disappeared after the restoration at the beginning of the twentieth century.

After several attempts of fusion, the first bell was cast in 1348 and installed in 1349 in the belfry. It was replaced in 1634 but this turned out to be imperfect. In 1666 the actual bell was put in, called summary (for the dedication to Maria Assunta) or bell by the Sienese people.

It weighs 6,760 pounds and because of its size it was installed above the cavity of the bell this time, where we can see it today. Even this, however, was not to be melted perfectly, despite being merged twice the previous year. Even today its sound is not uniform and varies according to where it is struck by the bell tower man. Being played traditionally only on the day of the Palio, its unique sound is associated with Siena's imminent feast. On all other days of the year, the hours are struck with an external automated hammer to the bell itself.

Up until 1379 the tower guard would even strike the time, but that year, it was replaced with a wooden automaton that, in memory of the first keeper, was called "Mangia" or "Eat". This automaton became metal in 1425 and then was replaced with stone. In 1780 it was replaced by the hammer cited, and the "Eat" stone is preserved today in the courtyard of the Palazzo Comunale Podesta. "

"Just think how much I've missed all this time. Is it possible that I haven't noticed any of it? The world was evolving all around me and I ... I didn't even notice a thing! Anyway, let's continue on our trip. "

I want to see the cathedral, climb up it and see the signs for the Duomo and Santa Maria; "Wait for me…I'm on my way!

What a beautiful square! Siena is full of all different types of unique artists!"

The Cathedral of Santa Maria del Fiore is the Cathedral of Siena. Built in the Romanesque-Gothic style, it is one of the most beautiful Italian churches built this way.

In the place where the cathedral stands, it would be built on Roman fort (Siena began as a Capitoline colony).

Even in the Middle Ages the name of it was Piano Sancte Mariae, and here, between where it currently stands and the square that surrounds it on both sides, they carried out the excavations that supported the hypothesis of a development in the area Lombard and frank period.

We're talking about a fortress with four towers, one of which would become the current bell tower. This building would be the residence of the Bishop up until 913 and would contain a church facing east, ie towards the present Baptistry. In the twelfth century this church was incorporated into the Romanesque building that was later to become the cathedral, its façade facing south, toward the current "Facciatone," the unfinished facade of the "new cathedral".

As also supported by historical deductions, it was tradition for the Dome to be consecrated on November 18, 1179. However, there are conflicting views and historical news that deny this date. In fact, only in the thirteenth century (1229) would it be turned into the basilica cathedral, its facade facing the west, toward Santa Maria della Scala hospital. The work was completed only at the end of the next century.

The dome was completed in 1263 and the Red padellaio is across from the "apple".

The present layout of the dome's apex dates back to 1667.

The '" Cathedral Worker " who oversaw the work being done was always chosen from among the canons, but from 1258 to the beginning of the fourteenth century, he was chosen among Cistercian monks of the Abbey of San Galgano. They were reported to be able administrators, so that the same City of Siena had entrusted the offices of Gabella and Biccherna (offices "revenue" and "outputs" of the Siena Republic).

It was the monks who called Nicola Pisano and his son John to do the work.

John worked on the facade at that time, using the marble facing on the bottom that we still see today. Nicola finished the pulpit in 1268.

The figure (perhaps from Cimabue) of Christ on the cross, with legs screwed, feet stacked and pierced by a single nail and "y-shaped" arms has become a classic in the world of iconography. It also appears to have been copied by the artists who created the recently-discovered frescoes in the crypt beneath the cathedral.

In 1313 the bell tower was finished, about 77 meters high. In 1316 the building was expanded under the direction of Camaino of Creswell, father of sculptor Tino Camaino.

As Siena reached its maximum splendor, it must have seemed that the cathedral was still too small for the city. He thought then to extend it so that the current nave became only the transept and the façade went back to its original position facing the south, placed much higher up than the ancient building. The project was given to Peter Lando (or "Lando Piero") following the decision of the General Council of the Bell on August 23, 1339. The work passed later under the supervision of the sculptor and architect John Augustine.

Because of the plague of 1348 and some structural collapse, work on the building was suspended in June 1357, leaving signs of failure in Piazza Jacopo della Quercia: columns footings and settings like those used to build the Museum of Metropolitan Cathedral, in addition to the unfinished facade (the "facciatone") from which we can enjoy a view of the unparalleled charming city. After a few years, they gave the work again to the master builder Domenico Augustine, Giovannni's brother, who died in 1366. In 1376, construction the top of the facade was headed by Giovanni di Cecco (called "John Stone"). In 1382 the vaults of the central nave were raised and that year may be considered to completion of the Duomo.

The large interior is in the shape of a Latin cross with three wide aisles. The the floor is made of marble, unique work of art in all of art history. The nave is topped with a ledge above which stand the busts of various popes (including that of Pope Giovanna).

The transept, including two aisles, has a hexagonal cross and is covered by a dome with a dodecagonal base, decorated with six large golden statues of saints. The whole of its parts is topped with a blind gallery decorated with small columns of patriarchs and prophet figures in chiaroscuro.

The pulpit inside Siena's Cathedral was built by Nicola Pisano from 1266 and 1269. It has an octagonal plan and an architectural structure and articulate with various reliefs and rounded statues instead of the columns at the top. Four of the eight columns at the corners rest on identical lions, while the center one lies on telamons. The arches are round-headed and three- lobed and there are marble figures that represent the virtues and a larger one with Christ above the capitals. The depicted scenes are the:
    * Nativity (exhibiting very soft lines)
    * Adoration of the Magi
    * Presentation at the Temple
    * Crucifixion (very dramatic - speech by Arnolfo di Cambio)
    * Slaughter of the Innocent Ones(attributed to his son Giovanni Pisano.)
    * Universal Judgement, joined together on both sides (attributed to his son John Pisano).

The floor in Siena's Duomo:

In classical antiquity, Sybil was a virgin who possessed prophetic powers seeing as she was usually inspired by a god, such as Apollo. Sybils, originally tied to rites inspired by Orpheus and Dionysus, usually gave obscure prophecies.

They lived in caves or in the vicinity of rivers and made predictions while in a state of unconscious frenzy.

There are seventeen Sybils, all belonging to legendary epochs and are divided into three groups: Ionic, Italic and Oriental.

The Piccolomini Library was built in 1492 by the Archbishop of Siena, Cardinal Francesco Todeschini Piccolomini (later Pope Pius III) to house the rich heritage of books collected by his uncle Pope Pius II.

It is located on the left aisle, before the transept, and was built over some circles of the rectory. It never housed the books for which it had been created. It was frescoed by Pinturicchio but only after the death of Pope Pius III. The frescoes describe events in Pope Pius II's life. It contains numerous valuable antiphonaries and the marble group of the Three Graces.

"Now let's go to Santa Maria della Scala":

Santa Maria della Scala is one of the oldest hospitals in Europe and one of the first examples of a xenodochium, which has not provided health services for quite some time now and was (and still is to some degree) the subject of a major overhaul for museum and cultural purposes.

This large complex, located in the heart of Siena across from the Cathedral, remains a testament to one thousand years of history, restoring an itinerary, from the Etruscan and Roman era to the Middle Ages and the Renaissance and now to the present day. In the artistic testimonies present here images of Etruscan civilization, tired pilgrims, travelers, sick people, noblemen, Byzantine emperors, abandoned children and praying monks are all mixed up together. In the museum monumental rooms, narrow corridors, frescoes with colorful stories of life, dark crypts, labyrinth tunnels dug in tuff and large vaulted-brick spaces are interchanged. Santa Maria della Scala does not lend itself then to a single interpretation, and although some of the greatest Italian artists will have left precious and rare examples, the large building (350,000 meters squared of which are open to the public) is primarily a fusion of the city and its history. Its uniqueness lies precisely in this very fact: it is a safe, where architecture, art and history tell a story of its very own that has continued uninterruptedly for a thousand years.

Built on the Via Francigena, it remains one of the first European examples of a combined shelter and hospital, with its own autonomous organization and designed to welcome pilgrims, assist the poor and shelter abandoned children. Its institution owes itself to the canons of the Cathedral, even if a medieval Sienese legend attributes its establishment to a mythical founder named Sorore, a shoemaker, who died in 898. The important complex was first said to have been managed by Cathedral clerics, then by hospital friars, gradually secularized and, in the fifteenth century, handed over to be controlled directly by the city. Thanks to the legacies of the great families the city and substantial donations that flowed into the coffers of Santa Maria, the hospital immediately earned an important place in the Sienese republic's economy in the territory where numerous agricultural properties were scattered, called granges, which has been for centuries a source of support for intensive hospital services. Santa Maria della Scala had an important role in this cultural environment, so much so that it was considered the city's "third artistic hub," along with the Public Palace and the cathedral.

The clientele's commitment to this prestigious institution in this artistic field proved to be constant from the very beginning, almost always the highest level and meeting all the needs of the millennial activity from the hospital: the great fresco cycle (unfortunately lost) with Stories of the Virgin painted by Simone Martini on the external façade, Ambrogio and Pietro Lorenzetti (1335), the series of frescoes in the great room the Pilgrimage, to the decoration of the vast apse of the church painted in the eighteenth century by Sebastiano Conca.

The original nucleus of Santa Maria is precisely the Santissima Annunziata Church, built around the middle of the thirteenth century, and expanded to its present size in the late fifteenth century.

Today the central focus of the Santa Maria della Scala museum exhibitions (of which 13,000 square meters are open to the public), however, is the Pilgrimage built in the second half of the fourteenth century and decorated almost a century later, an important series dedicated to the hospital's history. The Pilgrimage not only allows a significant opportunity for a historical and artistic reading to be made of a century cycle of great originality and beauty, but also recreates in detail the history and functions carried out by this century-old building. On large wall panels are, in fact, the institution's history and daily life inside the hospital are painted by Domenico di Bartolo, Lorenzo Oldie and Priamo della Quercia,

Since 1995, in addition to the church of Santissima Annunziata and the Pilgrimage, monumental rooms such as the Old Sacristy with paintings by Lorenzo Oldie, the Cappella del Manto with the bezel of Domenico Beccafumi, the Chapel of Our Lady, as well as rooms of the medieval barn that house the fifteenth century Fonte Gaia by Jacopo della Quercia, the striking local of the Society of St. Catherine Night and those of the historical site of the Society of Executors of Pious Provisions, the archeological museum and the large exhibition halls of Palazzo Squarcialupi have been progressively restored and opened.

"Truly a unique sight-to-see. I'm happy to be the only dinosaur to have seen such wonders.

The sun is rising now and the event will disappear all around us; but tonight at sunset, I'll go back to visit Siena, the city of a thousand colors.

Should I disappear, but where to?

This city has many tourists and many people who live there every day!

And if you find me, I'll become a freak!

Thank God I've found this guide. It's introduced me to this city's history.

I'll hide in the basement of St. Mary; yes, that's a good idea. "

And so, I found myself in places familiar to me, underground caves ... I was used to all that.

"Do you know how many things I've seen underground?
You can really see their Etruscan origins: below it's an entire archaeological find!
I hear the sounds of your daily life: people yelling, engines passing, machines working ... but how do you make all this noise?
Who knows!"
I was thinking if I fell asleep in the meantime, but I was afraid to sleep yet another million years and not to see everything around me then, I opted not to sleep and wait for the sun to set.
And the sun set!
I slowly walk out to see if the road has been cleared.

"Ok, I can continue my trip.
Since I'm here, I'll just jump over to the *contrade,* Siena's seventeen districts. Piazzetta of the forest so the district of the forest, one of the *contrade of* Siena. The others are: Aquila (Eagle) | Bruco (Caterpillar) | Chiocciola (Snail)| Civetta (Owl) | Dragon (Drago) | Giraffa (Giraffe) | Istrice (Porcupine)| Leocorno (Unicorn) | Lupa (She-wolf) | Nicchio (Shell) | Oca (Goose) | Onda (Wave) | Pantera (Panther) | Tartuca (Tortoise) | Torre (Tower) | Val di Montone (Ram's Valley).
It's easy to read all about it in the guide!"
Speaking of which: On July 2 and August 16 in Siena every year, in Piazza del Campo, The traditional Palio, which captures the city's attention for several days, takes palce; it is a bareback horse race (without a saddle) between the different districts of Siena. The Paleo is not exclusively a historical event or a reenactment of an ancient medieval joust, but it is the demonstration of the ancient and rooted Sienese tradition. It is very far from being an event that can be passed off in "a few days" but is the result of a precise and maniacal organization on the part of the city districts, whose members lead an active social life during the year.

The Palio attracts many tourists and is followed live by many television stations. The Palio has been linked to a lively controversy by animal rights associations who believe the race endangers the horses' lives. In addition, because of this public pressure, the city has recently increased its efforts to ensure a greater level of safety and support from the most-qualified veterinarians.

This controversy is partly due to the increasingly persistent attention that the media devotes to Siena's big celebration; accidents that eventually occur, in fact, are perhaps more in the spotlight as opposed to those that take place at the racetrack.

In Siena, however, the racing horses are well-cared-for and trained all year long. During the ninety-six hours of the Palio, they are the only ones able to bring the "rag" (sign of victory) to the district: The horse represents the *contrada* through the *spennacchiera* (the rosette with the colors of the district located on the front of the animal) and not the jockey, and ultimately, it is the horse thatwins the Palio which also is called "shocked" (meaning without its rider). In Radicondolithere is also a hostel for all Palio horses that can no longer run because of accidents or old age. One final note necessary in order to understand the Sienese veneration of this animal is it will not forget the name of a only horse that has participated in the race and to dedicate themselves more victorious graves where Contrada may render honors to these runners disappeared (such as the tomb of Brandano, a legendary horse of the recent Siena past).

"So much history and so nice to keep it alive.

Now, however, I got hungry ... it seems like I haven't eaten for centuries!

Millennia!

But I am in Siena, and although I am an herbivore and would not have a hard time finding a few shrubs and some tender leaves because there are all around, I want to taste the Siena's specialties.

I'd start with a nice ribollita with onions (cooked tuscan bread soup), then move on to cooked water, pici, roasts and venison with wild boar (thank goodness I was an herbivore!), panforte, Ricciarelli and pan'co saints.

All of course washed down with Chianti wine and *vin santo,* a dessert liquor "!

"Ah! That eaten"!

It would take a bit 'motion to digest everything. In Siena, they're ahead in sports, just take a look at not only the Robur and Montepaschi basketball teams, but also all the other sports Siena has to offer!

But because they are used to digest large quantities, I take this opportunity to four steps!

A visit to the Majesty of Duccio, the Archdiocese of Siena, at the Palais des papesse, the national art gallery, being careful not to fall in the works to wire the city with fiber optics!

And yet: the university, Monte dei Paschi, Siena's first bank and the first bank , the botanical garden, the Academy of Fisiocritici, the Chigi Music Academy, the Medici Fortress and a ear at Siena Jazz.

A look as well at Siena's palaces: Tolomei, Chigi Saracini, Salimbeni, the Captain ...Great!

"But in this city there are endless places to see:

Sanctuary of St. Catherine, Baptistery of St. John, Compliance, Santa Maria dei Servants, St. Dominic, St. Francis, San Bernardino, Synagogue, ports Siena: Sheepfold, Tufi, Roman, and Pispini Camollia ... there is to get lost!

I would have never imagined to have lived through an experience like that!

You're lucky to live in this paradise ... do not ruin it; in my day it was more difficult not to, although I miss that atmosphere and all my friends.

You are all here together in this magnificent place.

Live your life to the fullest.

Now it's time for me to get back to my ancestors but ...

I want to die right here; in Siena!

So I'll be not only with all my fellow dinosaurs but also in that very special place!

I've decided I'll go to piazza del campo; I'll rest there and ... if someone wants to come see me to say hi and share some thoughts ... just go up the Mangia Tower and

look at the square below.
You'll see my nine dorsal plates resting in the shadow of the tower.
Forever".

The End

Introduction

After being left by her boyfriend on Valentine's Day, Elizabeth decides to escape the usual monotony of her own everyday life, finding refuge instead in various "meaningful" places to contemplate her future and find herself.

She'll soon discover however that every place she visits will give her something unique and she'll relive old feelings from the past.

INDICE

Finito di stampare nel mese di Ottobre 2015
per conto di Youcanprint *Self-Publishing*

www.ingramcontent.com/pod-product-compliance
Lightning Source LLC
LaVergne TN
LVHW011602210726
843509LV00016BA/805